HOT REDEMPTION

HOT REDEMPTION

K.D. PENN

DRAGONFAIRY PRESS
ATLANTA

HOT REDEMPTION

This is a work of fiction. All characters, organizations, and events portrayed in this book are products of the imagination or are used fictitiously.

Cover artwork by Darren Davis
Space Age font by mickeyavenue.com
Font styling by J.N. Sheats
Chapter artwork by J.N. Sheats

Published by Dragonfairy Press, Atlanta
www.dragonfairypress.com
Dragonfairy Press and the Dragonfairy Press logo are trademarks of Dragonfairy Press LLC.

First Publication, December 2013
Trade Paperback ISBN: 978-1-939452-28-3
PDF ISBN: 978-1-939452-31-3

Published in the United States of America

Library of Congress Control Number: 2013946462

CHAPTER 1
EPIC

My dick pressed against my pants—hard, long, and ready— but it wasn't the nude girls dancing around me with luscious curves and jeweled skin that incited the erection. It was the hit—the guns my brothers and I wielded in our hands charged with siphons, the electronic currency stuffed in the pockets of drooling men who copped a touch of the dancers when the bouncers weren't looking, and of course, it was the rush of the quake I'd just snorted.

Heart-pounding music drummed in my ears. The song had a heavy bass and an omnichord melody. Something similar to the music I played before my criminal activities shifted from a past-time thing to a full-time necessity, prior to Mom's death, and well before Dad's mental demise. Our parents birthed ten kids. My brothers and I were the oldest. When Mom and Dad died, we became parents overnight.

Shitty parents.

"Epic, are you okay?" Toy nudged my shoulder.

I blinked and focused my artificial eyes on my brother. "Ask me that again and I'll fill that skull with siphons."

"You both keep your minds on the hit." Shade edged to the side and let me lead the way. His black skin made him look like a shadow in the darkness. He hid in the darkened club with ease. Unlike me. People always saw me coming first and didn't spot Shade until he jabbed his gun into their chest. I was tall with a muscular frame that scared people well before I threatened them. I'd been gifted with Mom's golden-tan skin and Dad's coarse blond hair that was thick and long like a lion's mane. Tonight it was pulled back in a band.

My siblings and I all had different combinations of hair and skin color because we were Unis. My ancestors had joined the Unified Movement hundreds of years ago in the 2000s. The movement believed that racism and discrimination would cease if all belonged to one race. People from different races mated together and their children mated with other mixed children, following the beliefs of their parents. It carried on for a century. By the 3000s, the movement had died down and a new race called Unis rose to the majority on earth.

Lot of good that did, being the Unis tend to be poor and live in impoverished sections of the planet. The minorities ruled.

"You didn't do any drugs tonight, right?" Shade tapped my arm.

"Naw," I said though quake coated my nostrils. I sniffed in the remnants of the bitter powder and wiped my nose with the back of my hand. The drug smelled like home. A sweet blend of melted butter, sugar, and vanilla all mixed in together. It reminded me of Mom.

How crazy is that? Quake reminds me of mom's cookies.

I laughed. Shade's dark forehead creased in the middle. "Your mind with us, Epic?"

"Always." The gun warmed in my hand. I kept it in my front pocket with my fingers wrapped around the handle. My pulse merged with the bass. I pressed the button on the butt end of the gun to charge the siphons. I imagined the glass bullets, no bigger than teardrops, trembling within the tunneled heat of the barrel. When I shot them, they'd burst through the air in a trail of bright light, pierce someone's skin, and explode.

Toy, Shade, and I prowled through the dark strip club with only the violet haze of light at the center to guide us forward. Women gyrated everywhere—on the laps of men, behind the shadows of thick curtains where the high rollers lounged, and on all the tiny stages propped in the corners of the rectangular club.

An olive-skinned girl danced on the center stage, rocking her curvy hips from side to side with fluid motion. Midnight-black hair hung down to her chin and curled at the ends. A glowing band of orange fabric wrapped around her full breasts. Amber gems, dangling in long chains from her red thong, gleamed with each flicker of light like sparks of a flame.

She's on fire.

At least it seemed that way, the more we moved forward. Five feet of space ran between her and us. The dancer's rocking shifted to a rolling of her body and twisting of oiled thighs. Back and forth. Around and around. She influenced her own groove and made love to the space.

Hypnotizing.

Her green eyes shifted to mine as if she'd heard my thought. She tossed me a wicked smile. One lathered in lusty promise and dripping with the willingness to give me whatever I craved. My dick twitched. I mentally ordered my eyes to snap a picture of her. It was something to look at later and help me find her again, when things were less conflicting. Light flashed from my irises, but no one noticed. Not many people had artificial eyes on earth. The surgery cost too much. So when light flashed around my face, most figured it was something else and ignored it.

But she noticed.

The dancer curled her finger my way and beckoned me over.

Not tonight. I winked. *But, damn, I wish I could give you a try.*

In a blur of motion, I pulled my gun out and shot the ceiling. Women screamed. The music stopped. Dust trickled down. My brothers targeted their guns at two bouncers, the only two that—we'd discovered a week ago—had actual guard training. The rest of the bouncers were just pudgy, tall college guys who appeared mean and tough, but with one shove in their ribs would probably cry like babies. Surprisingly, the dancer remained standing on the stage and hadn't run for cover.

"Time for the rich to give to the poor!" I waved the gun around. Dancers ducked. Men crouched to the floor. The bartenders in the back raised their hands in defeat. A door slammed behind us.

"What was that?" I asked.

"The college boy bouncers ran out the back exit." Shade grinned. "I won the bet. They left like cowards. You owe me a twenty."

"Lucky bastard."

"Just have my twenty in my hand by morning." Shade vanished back into the club's darkness. At night, the only time people spotted him was when he desired it.

"As if you'd ever let me forget." I shot another siphon into the ceiling. This time a slab of metal dropped down but didn't hit us. "Anyone else leave and they die! Let's make this quick, people. Fast and easy."

I backed up and let my brother host the rest of the party. Toy was a people person.

"We don't discriminate. All planets' currencies are welcome." Toy slung a big black bag on the center stage at the foot of the hypnotizing dancer. He returned his gun's focus back to his specified bouncer. "The lovely lady on the center stage behind me will be our collector. Get in a single-file line and dump your credit drives and copper disks in this bag that we've provided for your convenience."

"Only the guys need to donate." Shade materialized out of the darkness. "Ladies are welcome to hold on to their funds. You've all worked hard tonight."

A few women sighed. Shade winked at the redhead closest to him.

I took several steps back and leaned on the stage next to my hypnotizing dancer and the bag. I stared up at her. Most of girls would have shook in fear, but she wore a mask of amusement.

"Are you up for the collecting job?" I asked.

The wicked smile returned to her face. "That depends."

I quirked my eyebrows in surprise. "On what, sweet lady?"

"If I can take these heels off." She gestured to her feet.

I glanced at the glass shoes that arched up well above six inches. A thin beam of silver light served as the heel. It must have been all for show because there was no way the light provided support.

"Fuck. Those must hurt." I gained more respect for her dancing and made a note to check my sisters' closets when we got home. "How do you balance yourself in those things?"

"I'm very talented." Her leg brushed my arm as she slung off the shoes. Her flowery fragrance swirled around me, an aromatic blend of jasmine and rose.

Maybe I will *try her tonight.*

She squatted down and positioned the bag between her opened legs. I forced my eyes to remain on hers and not linger below her waist, to where I would surely get a view of her folds as they pushed against the thong's thin material. A line of grumbling men formed. One after another they hurled drives and disks into the bag. Electronic currency filled it and almost spilled over the rim.

When the line was almost at its end, I turned to her. "What are you doing tonight?"

"You mean besides crying into my pillow because all of my admirers were robbed?"

"I could give you another reason to cry into your pillow." I tossed her my own wicked smile.

"Only in your dreams, lover boy."

Toy chuckled in front of me.

The last man approached us, flung his disk into the back, and muttered, "May the Duchess of Light burn your soul."

"I doubt the Duchess would've liked you in here dolling out your funds to naked women," I countered.

"Let that be a lesson." Toy dipped his head and mock saluted. "We do the Duchess's heavenly bidding in our own way."

I smirked and would've laughed, if not for my hypnotizing dancer wrapping one of her amber chains around my neck. *Fuck.* My breath left me. Tightness constricted my throat. I gripped my gun and got ready to lift it. My vision blurred.

"Move your hands, lover boy, and it'll be the last thing you do," she hissed.

I wheezed and struggled to breathe. The gems cut into my neck, biting my flesh. It burned. Oxygen expanded in my chest, begging to be released. Pressure rose in my throat.

"Let him go!" Toy called over his shoulder. He was smart enough not to give the bouncer his back or we would all be dead.

"Slowly lift the gun to me, lover boy," she ordered. "Do it and you get to live."

With shaking fingers I complied.

You'll regret this later, sweetheart.

She yanked the gun from my hand and released my neck. Coughing, I shot up to grab it back. The hot point of the gun went to my forehead, burning my flesh. I jerked back and held in a shriek. For the first time in a while, fear shoved me into sobriety.

Her eyes showed no panic. She appeared comfortable holding a gun. "You sure you want me to rip apart that handsome face of yours with siphons? It really would be a waste."

"No. I'd like to keep my looks. It's the best thing I've got going for me." I raised my hands in defeat, but still, I was prepared to pounce on her at any opportunity.

"How are you getting out of here, pretty lady?" Shade's voice drifted from the darkness.

"Why?" She picked up the bag and slung it over her shoulder. "You need a ride?"

I inched her way. She shot me in the arm. The siphon gnawed through my skin at an insane speed. I gritted my teeth but didn't move. Blood dripped from the wound and then the bullet exploded inside a vein, ripping apart anything within in a five-inch radius. I collapsed to the ground and gripped the wound. The only good thing about her shot was that she only managed to hit the edge of my arm instead of the center where the whole limb could have detached.

"That's the only warning shot you're going to get." Her voice held an edge, but her fingers shook a little. No one but me could see it since I was so close.

It's just you, by yourself? Isn't it? No one watching your back.

I turned my face up to hers and snapped a picture. Light flashed. It shocked her. She shrieked and shot at my other arm. I dodged it. My body smashed into the floor. The rough carpet scraped the skin on my arm. More shots blared, probably Toy or Shade shooting. People screamed as they scrambled over one another, turning over chairs, racing out of the club, and searching for an escape. The smell of urine drenched the air. She dashed off, shooting out the violet lamps on the ceiling. Shattered pieces of glass rained down and sliced my skin.

The whole club turned dark.

"Fuck!" I jumped up, shoved running people out of the way, and shifted my eyes' view to night vision. Everything appeared light green. I caught a glimpse of one figure, female, and the only person walking calmly toward the entrance among the chaos. "She's five feet from the door! Head that way."

"Easy for you to say. We can't see shit!" Toy yelled.

"Follow my light." I switched my eyes to a white glow that illuminated two feet in front of me. It looked like I'd attached small flashlights to my head.

All three of us sprinted her way. She glanced over her shoulder. Horror shined from her green eyes. She raised her arm in the air and shot off another siphon. It exploded in the ceiling with a bang. Dust and metal fell. The crowd went even more hysterical, turned away from the front, and sprinted our way. She pushed through them, but I could barely follow her. Shrieking dancers bumped into me. A man slammed into my chest and screeched. Tears streamed down his face. I shoved him to the ground and hopped over him. More people pushed me back as they fled. All I could do was try and see where she was going.

My eyes captured something normal ones could not, being so far away and within darkness. A tattoo on her back. I snapped a picture and another and another as she burst through the front door, slammed it behind her, and disappeared into the night.

After a minute, we made it outside, but I knew it was too late. The cool night air chilled my skin. Old gas cars rushed past us on the street. Higher-tech vehicles sped by overhead. Whether she drove in the ground or air, we had no way of finding out. She was gone. There was no way around that.

"You get a pic of her?" Shade said between breaths. He bent over with his hands on his knees. Toy wiped the sweat off of his pale face with his arm. His red strands stuck to the side of his face.

"I got some images."

"Let's see if we can work with what you've got." Shade gazed at the aerial highway above us.

Nodding, I closed my eyes and flipped through my display. All the photos I'd taken tonight lined up in my mind—her dancing within an amber glow of flames, her shocked expression as she held the gun, and all the tattoo pictures.

"She has a tattoo. Looks like ink instead of electric thread." I mentally yanked out the ones of her tat.

"Ink? That should be easy enough to find her. We could hit up one of our cousins in Decker Park. They'll know all the ink artists." Toy stared at the aerial highway too. "Not many tattoo parlors still using ink, probably only five or so on the planet."

"What is the tattoo of?" Shade asked, as if already designing a strategy in his head.

I zoomed into the image. The tattoo stretched over her whole back. Orange and scorching-red flames began at the center and licked up the sides. Thick feathers existed within the fire. A bird's wings expanded at the top, as if it were climbing out of the inferno. The tips of the wings' edge were close to her shoulders. The beak pointed up as if the bird were targeting the sky.

"Of course." I laughed. "It's a phoenix flying out of flames."

CHAPTER 2
PHOENIX

As soon as I was behind the closed door of my shitty motel room, with all the locks securely in place, a huge grin spread across my face. Not even the rat nibbling a stale chip at the edge of the bed could blow my natural high. I reached down into the small bag my unwilling accomplices had provided me with and lovingly ran my fingers over the easiest money I'd ever made. The smooth surface of the disks slid against my skin. The smell of copper filled the air and overpowered the stink of filth in the room.

Pulling out a fist full of money, I let the rainbow of multi-planet currency fall over my body. It poured down on me. The hard metal disks and drives were welcome pain. *Make it rain, baby, make it rain.* That was the kind of rain a girl could get used to standing in. In no time I scooped the money up and tossed it back in the bag. Most of it had fallen to the green carpet. Dirt and something wet stuck to my hands as I scraped the money up.

"I'm moving into a new room tomorrow." I kicked off my heels, imagining a better hotel where the mattress didn't boast of blood stains, rats didn't crawl around the room when I turned off the lights, and the hot water worked as well as the toilet flushed. "Just one more night of this shit palace."

I laughed to myself as I remembered tall, blond, and horny's smug expression turn to total shock when I wrapped my string of jewels around his neck. Okay, there was no denying that in another time and place the night might have ended completely different for the two of us. I wasn't blind; the man had raw animal magnetism—the kind that made me want to climb on top of him just to see how long he'd let me stay there. *Alpha male meet me.* I would have loved the challenge of mastering him, even if it was for just one night, because someone like him was definitely the kind of guy a girl should throw back.

I'd learned that lesson the hard way from Teddy. Fear crept up my spine just from thinking of that name. My bottom lip quivered. My pulse raced. Even long gone, his name incited terror in my chest.

Stupid son of a bitch. I won't let thoughts of you ruin this high. You're dead. You can't hurt me ever again.

Flipping on the air conditioner, I strolled by my bed to the wall across from me. The air conditioner rattled and shook the wall as it blew out air. Torn wallpaper flapped back and forth. A little smoke lifted out from the vent, but the hotel manager said that was no big deal. Not that he was a trustworthy person. He'd offered me the option to give him a daily blow job instead of paying the regular amount. *An upstanding guy, that one.* I'd declined. But lately as my funds dwindled into single digits, I'd been considering that option, to my upmost regret. I'd even gone back into exotic dancing, which was how I spotted those three groovy guys and came up with the awesome and yet completely uninspired plan to take the money from their next hit.

I'd been watching the gang ever since I'd seen them hit another club I worked in a few months back.

That night, they'd stomped in, wielding guns and blasting siphons. Everyone dove to the ground, including me. Dread had rocked me into compliance. Who knew what type of men were robbing the place—killers, rapists, sadistic assholes that got off on torture and tears. I remained on the floor and did what they asked, but I kept my gaze on them too, just in case there was a moment I could escape.

They had marched to the club's center stage and forced a dancer to hold the bag while men stuffed it with their money. The dancer had pissed on herself. Urine soaked her thong and streamed down her thighs. The handsome blond leader cursed, yanked off his shirt, and helped her with cleaning herself up. I'd known right then that the guys weren't killers. A psycho wouldn't have cared and I knew psychos. At the end, they grabbed the money and rushed out of there, harming no one but the patrons' wallets, who'd come in for a hot night with half-naked ladies.

The next morning, I checked the news droid, which reported the Unis gang had struck again. Their names were unknown. Their faces from the club's video plastered all over the screen, but I knew that anyone who knew the guys wouldn't rush up to the police station to tell on them. The Unis population held a tight bond. They stayed in their communities and kept to themselves.

The club I'd worked at closed down due to the robbery. It so happens that the second club I worked at, they robbed too. And just like before, they had the center stage girl gather the loot and hand it to them. No casualties came from the hit. They stormed in, grabbed the money, and dashed out.

An idea uncoiled in my mind like a satin ribbon being unwound from its spool. *I'll rob them.*

So for weeks, I'd dance at night and research them during the day. They only robbed clubs not owned by Unis and they never hit the same club twice. That had narrowed it down to ten more clubs left for them to rob. Once I decoded their pattern, I had laughed about how simple it was—they hit clubs on busy nights and when not many bouncers were scheduled to work. I cased them for two months while they—completely unaware of me—robbed strip club after strip club, in and out. They were good. Each time they finished faster than before. I was impressed with their precision and skill, but unfortunately for them, I was better, or at least less predictable.

A woman always has the upper hand in those kinds of places. They never realized I'd been right there at the other clubs, even though I'd bumped into or stood right next to them many times. A woman has the ability to be invisible or be seen, depending on what she wants—she holds all the power.

Too bad for their bank accounts that they didn't get that memo.

After tonight I should have just enough money to buy the kinds of things I'd need to move on to bigger and better things.

Goodbye, earth with your chemical rains, mounting landfills that spread across countries, and pitiful excuse of a human job market.

My plan: find me a wealthy sugar daddy to pay my way off this shit-hole planet. The catch-22 of it was that most of the whales I had my eyes on weren't stupid. No, they'd see an ex-stripper like me coming a mile away. But…if I already had some money of my own…well, I'd be sitting pretty in no time.

My mind drifted back to the blond gang leader. Too bad I'd had to shoot him, but I knew I'd only get one chance at ripping them off. I'd spent too much of my time planning to be at the right strip club at the right time. I was tired of waiting. Besides, this planet was a study in Darwinism—he should have known better than to trust someone like me. And despite everything, I almost hadn't gotten away with it. It was those damn artificial eyes. I'd been prepared for them. I knew he would snap a few pictures of the dancers. *I mean, why wouldn't he?* It didn't matter. I'd still lost my shit for a moment—memories of Teddy with the same type of enhanced eyes battering at my nerves. Teddy would flash them right before he beat me. He loved to take pictures of his marks—the scars and burns, the gashes that were so deep at times I didn't think skin enhancements would heal them.

Forget about Teddy. He's gone, far away, at least six feet deep.

Taking off all my clothes, I collapsed onto the motel bed. The springs squeaked. Dust rose from the tattered sheets. The adrenaline of the evening was finally wearing off and exhaustion hit me hard. I crawled under the comforter and checked to make sure my extra gun rested under my pillow. A dirty mildew scent radiated from the fabric, but still, I sank into it as though the comforter were feathers encased in silk. *One day it will be.* I wrapped my arms around the bag that held the means to my future, clutching it to my chest. Tomorrow I would begin phase two of my plan. Tomorrow would be the beginning of my new life.

"Epic, isn't that fucking cute? She's all cuddled up with our money." An angry voice pulled me suddenly from the fog of my sleep. I kept my eyes closed and tried to control my breathing. I had no doubt who was in my dingy little motel room.

How the hell did they find me? And so damn fast?

I'd have time to ponder that later. For now the only thing I had time to worry about was walking away in one piece, with *my* money. I inched my fingers under my pillow and slipped them around the gun. Once the cold metal smoothed against my fingers, I waited and listened for the opportunity to lodge siphons in their skulls.

"Well, what are we waiting for? Grab our money and let's go!" the same deep voice demanded, lathered with impatience.

"Let me wake her up first. I want her to see who took it and understand why." The voice caused me to shiver. It had to be the blond leader.

"Is that even necessary?" A third voice sounded from the far right.

So all three of them are here. How did they get in without me hearing it? How did they bypass the locks?

The floor creaked, signaling someone was on the move. I mentally steeled myself and pushed up from my prone position as fast as I could, the gun extended in the general direction the creak had come from. The blond's face came into focus. In his right hand he held a gun. A metal bandage wrapped around his left arm where I'd shot him. Those artificial eyes flickered from blue to a reddish-orange color as they met mine. His lips turned up slightly at the corners. "Damn, if you're not a luscious sight in only a bra and G-string, holding *our* money." Light flashed from his eyes as he took a picture of me. "Is that my gun?"

"I don't know—is it?" I hissed.

"Those hard nipples pressing up against your bra are messing with my focus." He raked his gaze over my exposed skin as if daring me to stop him.

"It seems you're a little confused." My hand shook, but hopefully not enough for anyone but me to notice. I arched my back ever so slightly to keep his focus on my breasts, just in case. "This is my money and my gun, lover boy. Don't let the door hit you on the way out."

"Seriously, Epic. You're going let her talk to you like that?" the darkest guy asked.

Forming my lips into a smirk, I kept my gaze locked on Epic's face. I knew who was in charge in this crew and it wasn't the dark one with the temper or the red-headed guy at the door. It was blondie.

"So your name is Epic?" I leaned my head to the side.

"Heard your name was Phoenix due to the ink on your back. Nice to meet you." He extended his hand toward me as if to give me a shake. Epic grinned when he saw me grimace. *Point for him.* That's how they'd found me so fast. They'd tracked me by my ink. *Fuck, fuck, fuck.* Although, the fact that they were willing to let me live meant they thought I'd simply seized a convenient opportunity presented to me, not that I'd been planning on ripping them off.

"I prefer Nix."

"And I'd prefer you handing over my money," the dark one grumbled.

"Not happening."

"Come on, Nixie baby," Epic stepped closer to the bed, "just give us back our money and we'll leave you alone. I hate shooting sexy women."

They weren't killers, but I bet they'd kill me if I forced them. So easy. I could probably shove the money their way and they'd leave, no beating me up, choking, rape, or murder. All would be forgiven. I glanced down at the bag. *No way.* I was nothing if not stubborn. "Back up, Epic, or I'll shoot you again."

"Friends don't shoot friends." He pressed the button on his gun. It hummed as it charged.

"You're not my friend."

"My brothers never miss a shot. Three guns to one. What you think your chances are?" the redhead asked with a smugness in his voice that I wanted to blast out of him with my gun.

"I need this money more than you do," I responded between clenched teeth. Sweat trickled down my spine.

"I doubt that." His face shifted to a serious expression.

"I'm not giving it back."

"Yes. You are."

"No." I tightened my index finger on the trigger and Epic's face turned to stone. He glanced briefly at both brothers. Something passed between them as silence filled the air. My heart tripled in time. I knew they were about to make their move. All the guns charged in unison. They hummed and lit up at the tips.

"Don't," I whispered.

"Don't what, Nixie baby?" Some unknown emotion rolled across Epic's face and his eyes wavered between colors—burnt orange to pea green, bright red to lemon yellow.

I chose that instant to pull the trigger. Unfortunately, my aim wasn't the best. The siphon hit the ceiling. I shot again. Instead of going in his chest, the next one blasted into the same arm I'd shot at the club. The metal bandage caught it. The siphon lodged halfway in and then exploded. Bits of glass sprayed around us. I ducked under the covers, but still, jagged shards sliced the skin on my arm.

A string of curses reached my ears just as another shot rang out in the room. Excruciating pain surged through my system, radiating from my right arm. *Someone shot me.* The siphon seared a path into my flesh, tearing tissue around it. My gun slipped from my numb fingers and I collapsed onto the bed, clutching at the bag of money with my good hand.

Epic tugged on the bag and I curled my fingers into it like claws. "You can pry it from my cold, dead hands." I met Epic's astonished gaze and forced a smile. "Are you really going to kill me? I'm just a girl, after all."

"Just a girl, huh?" He pressed the barrel of his gun to my forehead at the same time he cupped the side of my face with his large hand. The coppery smell of his blood burned my nostrils. I couldn't help the tear that slid from my eye. I really didn't want to die, but I wouldn't beg and

I wouldn't apologize. I'd made a promise to myself after Teddy that I'd rather die on my own terms than live on anyone else's ever again. Epic ran his thumb slowly over my bottom lip. I fought the urge to bite it.

A smile tipped up his full lips as if he were reading my mind. "You aren't just *anything*, Nixie baby. You're definitely not just a girl. You're all woman."

Pure rage roared through my system. He was going to kill me—and he was smiling while complimenting me?

"Fuck you." I bared my teeth into a snarl.

"Maybe later, after we've cleaned up that arm."

His beautiful grinning face was the last thing I saw before lights exploded behind my eyes and everything went completely dark.

CHAPTER 3
EPIC

"Please, Dad." Tears singed my skin as they streamed down my face. "I can't. Not after Mom."

"Epic." He pulled me into him and wrapped those heavy dark arms around me. "It's better this way. With my death, you'll get a big check to last you and the kids for years—"

"We want you, not some damn insurance money." I buried my head in the crook of his neck like a little kid. Snow landed on my face and bare arms. I shivered, but not from the cold wind breezing by or the snow that stormed down on us. I trembled from the moment.

How I wished I was only a kid. Not the man I had to be, the one who nursed my mother when she was sick, feeding her watery celery soup with a spoon, cleaning her feces-filled adult diapers, and covering her with a thin sheet when she had finally escaped the pain and passed away. The whole time I took care of Mom, Dad worked three jobs to help us survive. When he rushed home that night between breaks to tell his wife he loved her and to kiss her cheek, I was the one who had to tell him she'd died. I was the one who witnessed him crumble to the floor and drown into an unending sea of heartbreaking grief. And yet again, I was the one who stood on the roof next to this man, my dad. A man that begged me with all his heart to let him kill himself.

"Don't cry, Epic. I'm worth more dead than alive," he whispered.

"But we love you." My bottom lip quivered.

"Love won't pay the bills, clothe you kids, get the twins their medicine each month, and help Mimi go to college." Dad released me. "And even if love did provide, when your mom died…she took all of my love with her."

"Don't say that. Please, Dad, don't leave us."

He tightened his grip on me. "Word of advice, son. Find a nice girl to settle down with, but make sure you only care for her a little. Don't love her too much. Life is complicated enough. Get a girl you can live without, so when the time comes and she dies, you move on. Don't fall for one that you can't live without."

He let me go. I stared at the roof's ledge. It was several planks of silver and attached onto the apartment building's roof with rope. Everyone who owned aerial cars used the roof as its launching pad and paid for designated spots to park each month. Some drunk had crashed his car into the ledge months ago. Now a gaping hole in the foundation and those pitifully rope-tied planks served as the ledge. The tenants and I had begged for the landlord to fix it and explained the area was a hazard. The landlord refused.

"Take care of them, son." Dad backed up onto the un-steady ledge. The planks quaked under his weight. Snowflakes *fell to his dark skin and landed on his blond hair. "Don't tell the others what happened tonight. Tell them it was an accident."*

"No." I ran his way and reached out my hand to grab him. A crack sounded as the planks broke under his feet. He fell, dropping down so many flights into the darkness. Broken silver and rope followed him.

"No!"

Without screaming or crying, he smashed to the pavement. Blood splattered the snow-covered ground below. From my view, his dead body looked like a sleeping bird. The blood pooling out on his sides resembled wings. And then he shifted into a huge bird. Fire blew up around him. He rose into the air, flapping his wings as the flames licked up at his claws. And then he flew away, soaring past the building into the gray clouds.

I jerked up in my crowded bed and screamed. I scanned the room to make sure it was my bedroom. All eight of my guitars hung on racks up on the wall—from the omnichord upgraded silver wire to the old acoustic one dad had given me for my birthday when I was a kid. Articles of my old band Chameleon and memorabilia of every performance stuck to the other wall. Mom had made it a point of collecting every club flyer announcing Chameleon's events, our concert tickets, any interview I did with a magazine from big publications to small local rags. She even held on to musical programs of my kindergarten guitar recitals and some of the old sheets of music I'd written, even the few songs that my brothers picked on me about and the band refused to add to our selection as they doubled over in laughter. I wasn't much of a songwriter especially when it came to the ballads. My stuff boasted of an edge and usually involved me screaming. But Mom had framed all those old song lyric sheets in gold frames—"Life is like a Wet Dog," "Eat my Flesh," "Pause and Piss," and the one that Shade bothered me about for days, "Penis Voyage."

Mom had clapped at them all and said I was the best. *Damn, I miss you, Mom. I'll have to tell Dad about that crazy dream. He'll . . .*

It took me several seconds to remember he was dead too. He'd committed suicide three months before by jumping off the roof. But sometimes I thought he was still around. I closed my eyes and clutched the little heart hanging on the chain around my neck. The locket monitored my heartbeats and made sure my stress didn't place me in the red zone.

Tears swelled behind my closed lids. I rubbed them away before they could fall down my face. It took two minutes to overcome the pain that gripped me. I checked to make sure no one stirred in their sleep as they crowded my bed.

Good. They'd just start worrying about me again.

Both of my twin brothers' feet dug into my thighs, but at least they hadn't wet the bed. My green-haired dog Turtle lounged on my other pillow, farting with every third snore. *He has such a hard life.* I scooted to the edge of my bed and realized one of the twins had in fact pissed in the bed. A wet yellow stain slicked against my calf. The twin closest to the stain was Andy.

I yanked my leg away and shook Andy's small frame. "Get up. You wet the bed. Clean it up."

"Turtle did that." Andy sank into a pile of blankets and covered his head.

"Still your responsibility. You wanted the dog." I shoved him off the bed. He dropped to the floor with a bang and shrieked. Black curls hung all over his head in disarray. He stomped off and mumbled something, but made sure it was just low enough that I couldn't hear him and get enraged.

I stretched my arms and brushed green strands off my chest. *Turtle must be shedding again. I'll have to shave it off. I don't have time to groom him every week.*

"Just one morning I'd like to wake up to a bed full of naked women."

"Ones that don't piss in the bed, right?" Toy rolled over at the end of the bed and yawned. His moppy red hair splayed out across the pillow. His long legs hung over the edge and his feet touched the floor.

"Why are you in here?"

"Because you put that sexy trek in my room." He nudged a sleeping Randy to the side and positioned his body more onto the bed. Nix's face flashed in my mind.

"She's not a trek." I rose. "And I thought you were sleeping in Shade's room."

"Shade's got two chicks in there and refused to share." He propped a pillow over his face. "And he wouldn't let me watch either."

"Then why didn't you sleep on the couch?"

"Your brothers built a fort there last night and the cats have been sliding down it all morning."

"My brothers, huh?"

"Clearly, I'm adopted. I'm the only civilized one of the bunch. How's your arm?"

I removed the metal bandage. A scar blossomed on the skin, hard and blood red, but nothing else. The pain had decreased into an ache that would leave as soon as I snorted some quake. "My arm is fine. It'll be brand new in a few days."

He propped a pillow over his face. "Good. Now let me sleep, man. I've got work at the diner tonight."

"My bad. I'm just talking in *my* room."

He groaned. I laughed but tried not to make too much noise as I got up. Tiptoeing, I arrived at my dresser and slid my top drawer open. A small tube, barely three inches long and full of quake, lay under my folded boxer briefs. The drug sang to me and promised to cloud out my bad dreams. Sighing, I dug my hand into the drawer, searched, and found it. The slick glass of the tube chilled my fingertips. Quake was cold because it was harvested within special craters found on Mars, a planet coated in ice. I gripped the tube. My nose itched in anticipation.

"You okay, man?" Toy watched me from the bed and let his focus go to my hand.

Does he know what's in it? I hope not.

"Go back to sleep."

"You want to talk about what type of dream would make you scream?"

"Yeah. Right after I take a dump in your mouth."

He blew out a long breath and rolled over. "Yep. I'm definitely adopted."

"Epic!" My sisters banged against my door in unison. The wood rattled underneath their knocking.

"May the Duchess choke in light. What!" I slipped the tube into my pajamas' pocket.

Can I just get a few minutes to myself?

All five of my sisters burst through my door, arguing with each other. Their voices rose high in the air and surely woke up the family living in the apartment above us.

"Mimi put us on punishment!" The triplets yelled and pointed their brown fingers up at her. I never knew how the triplets did it, but most of the time they spoke in unison as if their birthday wasn't the only connection between them. They spouted off more blame against Mimi, their auburn curls bobbing with the movements.

Frowning, Mimi carried my sleeping baby sister in her arms as she stepped closer to me. At fourteen, she possessed hips and other developed things that I'd prayed to the Duchess she would never have, but she got them anyway.

Which proves the Duchess of Light is no mystical goddess that has arisen from the dead. She's just a human that rules all the planets. Although I would never say that out loud. It was an offence to talk bad about the Duchess on any planet.

"Did you punish them, Mimi?" I slid my thumb against the tube of quake in my pocket.

"I took away their dessert and gave them extra chores." Mimi nodded. Her long blond hair hung to her hips. Like me, she had Dad's hair and Mom's golden-tan skin.

"She's not the boss," the triplets declared. "Tell her, Epic. She's not the boss!"

I rubbed my eyes and turned to Mimi. "Why did you punish them?"

"They painted your prisoner red and green."

I snapped my face to them. "Did you paint her?"

The triplets beamed. Each was missing two teeth in the top front row of their mouth. "We made her pretty."

"Your prisoner looks like a bloody Christmas tree," Mimi said.

I gritted my teeth. "She's not my prisoner."

"I'm sorry." Mimi sucked her teeth. "They painted your new girlfriend that's chained in Toy's room with tape around her mouth, red and green."

"She likes it," the triplets declared.

Ignoring Mimi, I directed my attention to the triplets. "Mimi is right. All three of you are on punishment. No dessert tonight and you clean the kitchen after dinner."

"What?" they began to protest.

"We don't paint people." I stepped forward. Their mouths closed. Although they were only six, they'd lived hard lives. They knew when to fight and when to shut up and deal with it.

"Go get towels, soap, and water for my . . . guest." I caressed the tube inside my pocket with my fingers.

"Guest?" Mimi smirked as the triplets marched away with frowns plastered on their faces. "Do you think this is the proper thing for us to see?"

"You all aren't supposed to be in my room," Toy growled from under the pillow.

"Who is she?" Mimi rolled her eyes. "Did you all kidnap her? Why would you put her in chains and wrap her mouth with tape?"

So she wouldn't kill and rob us all.

Mimi spotted Nix and saw an olive-skinned beauty with haunting green eyes and the appearance of a delicate manner. She didn't understand that Nix was danger wrapped in a tight dress.

"Mind your business," Toy yelled.

"I live here too." Mimi pouted.

"Both of you be quiet. And, Mimi, we're taking care of this," I said. "Don't worry about it. She'll be gone by the afternoon."

Mimi shook her head. "It's not proper. The girls will think it's okay for their boyfriends to chain them up—"

"No one's having a boyfriend!" I targeted her with my eyes. "Let's make that clear right now."

"We're not talking about boyfriends. We're talking about chaining women."

"Still," I growled, "no one's having a boyfriend."

"And if one of us already has one?" She tilted her head to the side.

"If I see a guy near you, I'm loading him with siphons."

"I hate you!" She pouted and stomped off like everyone else.

I'll have to visit her school. Surprise this idiot guy during lunch. Maybe bring Shade along so the kid can wet his pants in the cafeteria in front of everyone. I laughed at the thought and then frowned at how upset Mimi would be if we did it. *I'll have to do something else. Something that will keep the kid away from her, but not point to me being responsible.*

"This is a record," Toy said from the bed. "You've managed to piss off five of our brothers and sisters in only fifteen minutes of being awake."

"Shut up and go back to sleep."

The tube of quake vibrated in my hand, but I couldn't attend to it at that moment. I had a date with a Christmas tree. The triplets claimed Nix loved her new look. I doubted it. Besides, it was time to tell her why we'd dragged her back to our place. Nix would be a vital component in our last hit. I'd explained that to my brothers last night when I rationalized why we were taking her. I planned on giving her the opportunity to join. If she said no, then I'd drop her off wherever she wanted.

She won't say no.

She had nothing. I knew breeds of roaches that would've cringed at crawling in that motel she slept in. My heart broke to see it. She deserved better—silk sheets caressing her skin, diamonds draped around her neck, and chocolate delicacies between those slender fingers. My dick clenched with hunger at the thought of those soft hands. I paused in the doorway and shut my eyes tight.

She's a possible partner on a job, not a bedmate. Concentrate.

I stepped into the hallway. The triplets stood on my right, shivering behind Mimi with gaping mouths.

"What's wrong?" I asked.

Mimi pointed to my left. I turned that way and gazed into the barrel of a gun that was held by red-and-green fingers.

"Playtime's over. Give me a reason why I shouldn't shoot you . . . again," Nix hissed.

I swallowed. "It'll traumatize my sisters."

"You mean the little cretins who decided I was full of Christmas cheer?"

"How did you get out of the chains?"

"Me and chains had an intimate relationship once. We broke up, now we're just friends." A murky gloom shined over her eyes for a second. It quickly disappeared, but my artificial eyes caught her pain. *Someone hurt her.* I hoped I could meet the person who harmed her. They would be dead in seconds.

I tilted my head out of the barrel's view. "I got a job for you. It'll be lots of money."

"I don't need a job now that I have *my* money back." She gestured with the tip of the gun to her feet. The bag from last night's hit sat by her toes. She'd kept the bandage I put on her arm from when Shade shot her. It didn't seem like it hurt much.

Shade crept up behind her wielding two guns. She had no idea. He made no sound and unfortunately wore no clothes. *God, we're shitty parents. If this altercation between Nix and me doesn't scare the girls, Shade's nudity surely will.* He'd just got penal beading last week. Thirty beads pushed up against the skin of his erect cock. The big thing resembled something diseased and bumpy, but the ladies loved it. At least that's what he claimed.

"Give me a chance to explain the job to you."

"I've got plans of my own, so no, I'm not interested in working with you." Nix shrugged, still not realizing Shade was behind her.

"No one's watching your back." I shook my head. "You think you can survive by yourself?"

"No one's ever not alone. The only person you can ever really count on is yourself."

"You'll be dead in a year. You need someone at that sexy rear, making sure it's safe."

"I don't need you or anyone else to watch it."

Shade placed the guns on her back. "You sure about that?"

CHAPTER 4
PHOENIX

I ignored the voice from behind me and kept my gaze locked on Epic. An already familiar smile tipped up the corners of his mouth, making me want to claw it right off. He was so full of himself, and it rankled me. I was still pissed that he and his gang had gotten the drop on me in my motel room last night. And to add insult to injury, I was now covered in red-and-green paint.

Imagine my shock that morning when I opened my eyes to three identical redhead little monsters painting my face. They giggled as they lathered my skin with cold paint. The thick liquid made me shiver. I tried to talk through the tape stuck to my mouth. They held single fingers to their mouths, told me to shush, and then returned to painting me as they sang Christmas songs. While the evil cretins had fun, I studied the room serving as my prison. Posters of famous actresses stuck to the walls. Most of the women wore tight, form-fitting clothes. I figured it was a guy's room and wondered if it were Epic's.

Once the teenage girl entered the room and spotted the triplets painting me, she rushed them out. Her gaze went to my chains. I struggled to say something. She shrieked and left me alone in the room, which was perfect. I could get out of chains in no time when left to my own devices.

Twin boys with black curly hair stepped out into the hallway. They couldn't have been more than eight or nine. A shaggy green-haired dog trotted out with them.

Are all these kids his and his brothers'? Clearly they don't know how to keep it in their pants.

"You and your crew ever hear of birth control?" I narrowed my eyes at Epic. The teenage girl laughed behind him.

"What?" His jaw dropped open in surprise. "You think the kids are ours?"

I raised my eyebrows at him and quirked my head. "Yeah, that's what I implied by my question. You're not very smart, are you?" It was a shame too, because he really was a magnificent specimen of a man. It was the first time I'd seen his long blond hair loose and not pulled back out of his face. My red-and-green fingers itched to run through the luscious locks to see if it would feel as soft as I imagined it would.

"Siblings, not my kids! They're my siblings," Epic snapped. "And I'm not stupid."

I grunted in response, because I'd just been wondering that. "This doesn't need to get ugly. I'm just going to walk out of here and forget I ever laid eyes on you."

"Not with *our* money." The voice came from behind me again.

"I stole it fair and square. Deal with it," I stated to everyone present.

"And we stole the money and you last night. Does that mean you belong to me now?" Epic had the nerve to smile at me again. I ground my teeth together.

"Nobody owns me." My nostrils flared against my will. My temperature rose to boiling. Teddy had tried to own me, and I'd made him pay for that mistake with his life.

Cold metal pressed up against the back of my neck. "Drop it, or I'll drop you, sweet lady."

"Tell your brother to take his gun from my back."

"Shade does what he wants." Epic crossed his arms over his chest.

It was time to fall back on the age-old trick used by many women everywhere. Cry. I wasn't above using it if the tears helped me out of a tight spot. I forced myself to think about something really sad. *Dying puppies. Think about dying puppies and people clubbing baby seals.* Yep, that did the trick every time. My lower lip trembled. My vision blurred.

"Please," I whimpered. Huge, fat tears escaped from the corners of my eyes and tracked down my cheeks, dripping to my shirt. "I really need the money. Just let me have it and you'll never see me again."

"You don't expect me to buy that, do you? I have sisters." Epic laughed and shook his head.

Time to turn up the heat.

I hated thinking about him, but at least I got something out of our twisted relationship—a way to give myself an instant panic attack. I pictured Teddy, the way his dark eyes glittered at me when he had been torturing me—branding me for his, the sharp tip of his knife, the sting of his teeth when he bit into my flesh, the sound of his lighter when he flicked it on and off, taunting me with the possibility of fire. My breaths began to come in short little spasms, my heart pounding so loud I couldn't hear anything else. Images of him wielding a long flame flashed in my head. I gritted my teeth. Sweat streamed down my face. I knew what I must've looked like—pathetic, scared, and lost. But the emotions were authentic and therefore Epic wouldn't be able to deny them as the truth.

"Let's go in the back," the teenaged girl carrying the baby said as she guided three young little redheads down the hall and away from the scene.

"But she's so sad," the girls said in unison.

"Epic will make her feel better." The teen shoved them along.

"Shade, lower the gun." Epic motioned with his hands.

"You're going to let her go? With our money?" It was Shade's turn to sound incredulous. I kept my attention directed to the floor and battled with myself to not smile.

"Does she look like she's in any shape to go anywhere?" Epic asked.

"You have a point, but that doesn't mean she can take my money," Shade argued.

"Move the gun, man."

The cold metal of the gun disappeared from my skin. It took me only a moment to push the memories back down into their locked box so I had control of myself again. Once my breathing evened out, I whirled around to point my gun at—a completely naked Shade. *Why is it my eyes always seem to go to the one place I wish they wouldn't?* My eyes widened as I stared in complete shock at Shade's disgusting-looking dick.

"Wha-what the hell is wrong with your dick?" I stammered. Bumps covered it, and the bumps were huge. He had a big one, I had to admit, but that didn't stop his dick from looking like it had some kind of weird disease.

Shade tried to wrench the gun out of my hand, but my grip was tight and held fast. Epic grabbed me. It felt like two large bands of steel wrapped around my body, pinning my arms down to the sides.

"Nothing is wrong with my cock. I got beaded enhancements under the skin." Shade glided forward and pried the gun from my hand.

"Why would you do that?" I scrunched my face in horror. There was no need to stress about being found out for faking. They already had my gun. And Epic's hold on me was unyielding. I'd need super strength to break out of his arms.

"The beads vibrate when it's surrounded by warmth." Shade grinned. "The ladies love it. My beads rub against all of their favorite sides and make them come in seconds. You want a try?"

"No way." I struggled in Epic's arms. He pressed my back against his hard chest. Shade chuckled to himself and backed away.

"I can't believe I almost fell for that," Epic murmured in my ear. His voice was low and sensual, eliciting a reaction from my traitorous body. It'd been months since I'd had anyone worth remembering between my thighs. That fact combined with the very manly, spicy aroma that was emanating from Epic had me contemplating other ways to separate him from my bag of money. I thrashed about and tried to wriggle free in his arms, while very conveniently wiggling my ass against his crotch. I didn't want to make it too obvious, but I knew I was doing the right thing when a low groan left his lips. His hardness pushed up against my behind.

"Let me go," I growled—okay, more like purred—but hopefully I would be the only one who could tell the difference.

"I think you and the chains are going to have a surprise reunion," Epic rumbled.

Oh fuck no. I wasn't getting chained up again. That's when I began to fight in earnest.

"No!" I screeched. "I'm not going back in those!" I did everything in my body to get out of Epic's arms—kicked, scratched, tried to head-butt him, but he didn't let me go and all I got was exhausted and aggravated.

"Fuck, she looks like a crazed kitten. Need any help with her?" Shade chuckled some more. "I'm good at taming kitties."

"No. I got her." I could hear the smile in Epic's voice. He turned me around and I managed to knee him in his impressive erection. A shame, really, but I wasn't going back in those chains.

"Fuck." He grunted and finally let me go. I grabbed the money bag and sprinted down the hallway. A friggin' ton of bricks hit me from behind and knocked the air out of my lungs. I crashed to the ground. The impact of my body hitting the carpet hurt so much I cried out in pain.

"You're not going anywhere." White teeth flashed in Shade's dark face as he turned me over and dragged me back toward my doom. His bumpy monstrosity rubbed against my legs.

I jerked away from him with dread. "Control that thing."

"Not even I can control it." Shade winked.

"I think I just threw up a little in my mouth from your oversized ego. It's about to get worse if you don't back off."

"You throw up in this hall then you clean it up." Shade lifted me like I was a feather, slung me over his shoulders, and rushed me back into the room I'd been locked up in all night. I still hadn't quite caught my breath by the time I realized I was back on the same bed, in the same chains I'd managed to escape from earlier.

"Fuck," I rasped. "These won't keep me. You know that, right?"

"Say you'll give me a few minutes to explain the job to you without shooting me in my arm, taking my money, or ramming your knee into my precious balls," Epic limped into the room slightly hunched over, "you promise that, and I'll take them off of you right now."

I bared my teeth at him. "I told you, I already have plans."

"Not anymore you don't, if the bag of money is part of your plan. You want out of those chains—agree to listen to me."

Back to my seduction strategy.

"Maybe you and me can come to some other kind of arrangement." I rolled my hips off the bed seductively. "How about asking him," I flicked my eyes in the still-very-naked Shade's direction, "to leave, so we can, you know, talk?"

"Don't do it, Epic." Shade waved his hands from side to side. "That kitty has claws and is definitely going to scratch the shit out of you."

"I'll play nice, I swear. Unless you don't want me to." I bit my lower lip and let my gaze run over the length of Epic's large body. *Yeah, I could play nice with him to get what I want.* Epic scrubbed his hand over his face and his eyes turned from ice blue to burnt orange.

"Why do your eyes shift to different colors?"

"They change with my mood." He directed those flaming-orange pupils my way.

"What does orange mean?"

"I don't know." Frowning, he blinked and his eyes transformed back to blue.

"It means he's horny." Shade laughed. "Are you sure you don't want help with that kitty?"

"No. Maybe I like claws," he muttered.

"Your body." Shade left and slammed the door behind him. *Immature much?*

"Unlock these chains, so we can talk," I cooed.

But Epic stayed where he was. "First you knee me in my junk, and now you want to what—kiss everything and make it better? What's your angle now?"

Ignoring his questions, I lifted my ass off the bed in invitation. "Only one way to find out."

Epic moved forward with the grace of some kind of large predator. I swallowed. My nerves jittered about. I gripped the sheets next to me, not liking the vulnerability the chains forced me into or the possibility that I couldn't tame this huge man. When he came to sit next to me I arched up my head toward him.

"Unlock me, and then we can play." I licked my lips and watched his eyes follow the movement.

He chuckled to himself. "First a kiss, and then I'll release you."

"No—"

He brought his index finger up to my mouth to silence me.

"I have the key, I make the rules." His eyes glittered with amusement as he seemed to be waiting to see what I'd do next.

"Fine," I grated. "One kiss, and then you unlock me."

He leaned forward, inch by inch, and my breath hitched. Damn if I kind of really wanted him to kiss me. *What the hell is wrong with me?* Maybe I had a concussion from being knocked out last night? Yep, that could explain it. I wasn't thinking clearly at all.

When our lips met, an undercurrent of electricity coursed through me, emanating from the point of our connection. I heard myself moan in pleasure as his tongue slipped into my mouth to tentatively explore. He tasted sweet and masculine both at the same time, and raw lust pulsed in my core. *Having sex with Epic . . . well would be epic.* I internally giggled at my joke just as our kiss deepened. I welcomed the abrasive feel of Epic's unshaved face as he pressed into me more aggressively, a groan escaping from his mouth to mine when I nipped at his tongue.

In seconds, the full weight of his body was suddenly on me, trapping and confining me to the bed. A sliver of cold panic slid into my heart, serving as ice water to my system. I had no control with him on top of me, and even worse, it reminded me of another, one that haunted my nightmares. I reached the end of the chains but still managed to push at his massive chest and break our kiss.

"We kissed. Now unchain me." I hissed into Epic's much-too-close face. Even though I felt trapped and weak, it was so hard to think with his hard body pressed into mine. It took everything in me not to grind against him and ask for more. He dragged himself off me slowly and then walked away from the bed. He muttered something under his breath.

"Where are you going? To get the key?" I asked with hope, but I had a sinking feeling in my stomach, one that told me I was about to be played.

"I changed my mind." Epic's voice cracked, an octave lower than normal. He placed his hand under his shirt and clasped his fingers on to whatever little ornament hung on his chain. "I don't think I can trust myself around you if you're not in chains. I can barely deal with you *in* them."

Without another backward glance, he slipped from the room and shut the door securely behind him.

"You fucking asshole!" I screamed after him. "We agreed! Let me the fuck out of here!" But no answer came.

CHAPTER 5
EPIC

Nix stepped out of Toy's bedroom in a clean pair of jeans and a shirt that formed tightly around those full breasts. Mimi had given her the clothes and was also the reason why Nix wore no chains. After I escaped from Nix's sweet lips, Mimi had cornered me in the hallway and yapped me into humiliation. She accused me of being an abusive captor and a sadistic torturer. For added measure, she claimed mom was watching and full of shame at my behavior. I unlocked the chains, gave Nix some clean clothes to change into, and waited in the living room with everyone else to do the last thing Mimi demanded.

"Hello, Queen Nix." I did a dramatic bow. Mimi hit my back and Nix smirked.

She probably thinks she has some sort of power now. Whatever.

As far as I was concerned, the best part of this moment was the sight of Nix's thick hips in those much-too-small jeans and her breasts bursting out of the shirt. The top of the material looked like it would rip within seconds if she coughed or breathed too hard. I hoped for both as Turtle ran into the room and collapsed on our deer skin rug.

"Go ahead," Mimi whispered behind me and patted by back.

"Nix, we are very sorry." I formed fists with my hands where they rested in my pockets. "We now agree to give you one fourth of the money due to our behavior."

"Only one fourth?" Nix's black eyebrows rose. Her sensual lips changed into a sneer.

She'll regret that remark later. As soon as I get her out of here.

"One fourth is all we can give up right now." I directed my attention to her breasts and blatantly snapped a picture. The flash burst from my irises. Yet perky nipples stiffened under the fabric, begging to be licked and sucked. I trailed my tongue along the top of my lip, just thinking about them. *What color are those plump points, bright pink or a darker shade of her olive skin?* I heard an intake of breath from her way. Once again my dick hardened—that seemed to be its only action when I was around her. She gazed down at my jeans.

You see what you do to me, don't you?

I winked. "Your turn, Shade."

Dressed in his dark green automotive repair coveralls, he remained where he was. Mimi cleared her throat. A rumble thundered from Shade's chest as he stepped forward. The triplets giggled on our black couch while they watched with everyone else.

Shade mumbled something.

"I'm sorry. I didn't hear that." Nix leaned his way and cupped her hands around her ear.

"Go fuck yourself." Shade turned around and stormed off.

"Shade!" Mimi got in front of him and placed her hands on her hips. "I swear to God, Jesus, and the Duchess of Light, I will not fix the cooker or the cleaning robot if you don't be nice."

He faced her. "But—"

"I'm so serious. I mean this is ridiculous. You're older than me." Mimi tapped her foot.

Shade's face snapped to Nix. "I, too . . . am sorry."

"For what exactly?" An innocent expression spread across Nix's face. If I hadn't known the situation, I would have believed the act. *She's perfect for the job. I have to get her to agree.*

"I'm sorry for threatening you with my guns and showing you my . . . special beaded guy," Shade barked. Everyone laughed. Even I had to cover my mouth to stifle a chuckle.

Too bad Toy's already at work. He would love this.

"Thank you." Nix bowed at Mimi and curtsied at the kids. They all clapped and cheered as if she'd just slayed two dragons.

I bet they would love to hear us tell them sorry *every now and again. Not going to happen. What had Nix called them? Cretins, I think. I like that.*

Mimi handed Nix a small silver container shaped like a grape. Two red dots raced within the metal and circled it over and over "I transferred your portion of the credits over to this mini-bank and programmed your DNA as the password. I lifted the DNA from your old clothes. Sorry."

"Umm . . . thanks?" Nix quirked her eyebrows. "How do I work this thing?"

"I cleaned the currency so there is no trace to whoever the guys borrowed it from." She pressed the center of the container. Red glowing dots emerged all over the surface. "You can take this in any store, business, or bank to buy stuff or transfer the funds over to your account. Press both sides and it gets smaller."

Just like Mimi said, the metal grape decreased into a coin. "Press it twice and it goes back to its original size."

Nix's green eyes widened in amazement. "And if I happen to misplace it?"

"Or even if some arrogant buffoon tried to take it back." Mimi glanced my way. "They can't. It's drawn to your skin like metal to a magnet. It makes robberies impossible."

That invention was why my brothers and I kept hits to illegal strip clubs where everyone was mostly human and the places only took electronic currency that could be nabbed and retraced by any smart techie. New technology was making burglaries harder. Soon it would be impossible to steal without being familiar with computer and robot systems.

"Damn, you're a genius, kid." Nix turned the mini around in her hand. "Did you put this together all by yourself?"

"Yes." Mimi's smile widened. "I always get an A in all courses dealing with cybertronics."

"Is that what you're planning to major in when you're old enough to go to college?" Nix asked.

I cringed at the mention of college. All colleges cost too much. One semester of Mimi's education would set the whole family back a year. *But she has to go.* Regular human labor jobs that required a high school education were nonexistent on any planet but ours. An individual couldn't make minimum wage without at least a bachelor's degree. Nowadays people built robots and created complex systems to control the robots more efficiently.

Machines did everything else. Those circuit devils packed every factory and plant, making anything that could pass on an assembly line, managing the electronic workers, and loading the docks. They cleaned everything from houses to companies, streets to cars. Few jobs existed for humans, but there were some present—landfill loaders, drug dealers, sex industry workers. Fortunately, old people still refused to use robotic doctors, food service workers, drivers, and child care providers. There'd been reports of robots botching surgeries and lacking in the emotional development department to take care of kids. Plus, a lot of the older generation preferred human-run businesses, but in twenty or so years they would all be dead and the cyber industry would dominate.

Mimi needs to go to college, and the other kids too.

"So nice to meet you all." Nix shook the triplets' hands. "Next time use some different colors for the future prisoners. Branch out and get inspired."

The triplets giggled. Nix high-fived the twins.

"Alright, Nixie baby. Let me drop you off at your motel." I reached her, hooked my arm around hers, and towed her toward the door.

She attempted to climb out of my grip. "No, I'm good. It looks like I can afford an air taxi now that my financial situation is suddenly looking up."

"Oh no. It's really not a problem for me." Opening the door and yanking her out, I quickly shut it behind us and slammed the cuffs on her wrists. "Scream something and you go back in my apartment. Mimi and the kids would love to have you spend the night."

"First chains. Now handcuffs?" She stared at the thin lines of blue light clamping her wrists together. "I suspect a fetish. What's next? Planning on taking me to one of those silicone dungeons where fat nerds beat their pricks to big-breasted androids?"

I wrenched up my shirt to show her the layers of muscle wrapped around my waist. "Do I look like a fat nerd to you?"

She concentrated on the area longer than I thought she would and bit her lip. I released my shirt. It rolled down my body and she watched it drop. *What are you thinking about?* The very possibility of lusty thoughts swarming through her mind about me caused me to shiver.

"What do you want?" A sultry intensity laced her words. It sounded so good I almost shoved my hands into my pants to touch myself.

I bet she could make me come with just her voice alone. I shook my head. *She's too dangerous to touch. Keep it all business.*

"Let me explain the job to you while I take you home." I led her down the lime-green hallway and assumed her lack of smart remarks or physical resistance was a sign of her compromising. Sensors lit up around the entrance to the roof. The one in the center scanned my eyes.

"Proceed." The female voice sounded.

The door opened. Hot air rushed in. *Good old Earth.* When it wasn't a blizzard, the sun beat down on the planet without restraint. I resisted the urge to look in a particular direction, like the spot on the roof where my dad killed himself. Although it had been months, the landlord just fixed the ledge last week. But, still, I couldn't look.

Towering glass buildings surrounded us. Tons of people lifted off their roofs in aerial cars and bikes. Barely anyone drove electric or gas cars, unless they were teenagers with a learner's permit who were restricted from driving high or the old generation that fixed up and polished vintage sports cars and cruised around in them on a sunny Sunday afternoon.

I kept my back to the area. "I'm parked over here."

"I hope you're not referring to that metal monstrosity over there charading as a bike."

"Don't be so mean. She's beautiful." I laughed. My metal temptress relaxed far away from the other vehicles. A sleek gray paint covered it and shined in the sunlight.

"No way am I getting on that," Nix said when we approached it.

"Diamond is safe." I patted the leather seat and slid my hands up against the metal hump in front of it, thinking of the many memories that came from that hump. Many women sat on that spot and enjoyed that area most of all. I glanced at Nix. *I shouldn't do this. I should just have her sit behind me like a regular ride.* I swiped a peek at those juicy melons pushing against her shirt. *Damn the Duchess. I'm going to hell anyway.*

"Hop on the front." I patted Diamond's hump. "Don't be scared, Nixie baby. I'll go as fast as you allow. You'll control the speed. Okay?"

"I'm not scared." She glared at me in defiance before she jumped on. I held back my grin and got behind her, maintaining an inch of space between us.

I better tell her about the plan now, because once Diamond starts, Nix will be preoccupied.

"You ever been to Trinity?" I asked.

Her whole body tensed in front of me. "Never. It's expensive to get a transport ticket to that planet, even more to stay there for a few nights. But a girl can dream . . . some pretty big whales live there. I'd love to cast my line and see what mama could reel in."

Sugar daddies. I never pegged her for that type.

Rage coursed through my veins and would've short circuited my eyes if I hadn't calmed myself down. I didn't like the idea of creepy rich guys touching her just because their pockets were stuffed. If someone was going to stroke her soft skin and it wasn't me, then I wanted it to be a man who deserved her.

"Sooo . . . what about Trinity?" Her voice held anticipation.

"A strip club named Dynamics opened up three months ago. I got a job as a bouncer there through a cousin that lives on the planet. I start in two days. I've seen vids. It's plush with three dance levels and two floors of private rooms. All types of dancers—human and androids with flesh so close to ours it cost more to rent them for the night than a real female." I slid my key card in the ignition slot. Diamond warmed, but hadn't begun to rumble yet. "My cousin checked out the spot. He claims it's bringing in two million a night."

"In what currency?"

"Trinity's cube, of course."

On any planet that wasn't earth, people used the electric dollar to buy gum for their kids or to give to a homeless bum on the street. The cube topped all currency in the galaxy. One cube was worth a hundred earth dollars.

"My brothers and I robbed a lot of night spots on earth to save up for a move to Trinity. Tomorrow, we transport the whole family to a house in the working class section of the planet," I said. "We stole enough money to keep us there for two months. If you join the job, then you'll get a ticket and a room for two months in our house."

"What part would I play?"

I imagined the calculations breaking down in her head. We could all walk away with half a million cubes each. With that money, she could run off to a more cost-effective planet and provide for herself until she died. There would be no need for sugar daddies or reeling in whales that didn't deserve her.

"I'd get my cousin to get you a job as a dancer there." I licked my lips. "One look at your face and the way you rock those hips, you'd be hired in seconds. Once you're in, I need you to get a layout of the performers' changing areas and anything else you can think of. When the guys hit the club, we'll have you collect the money in a bag like the other night. You'll act like you're scared and we'll take you as a hostage to make sure no one tries to blast us as we leave."

Silenced passed as Diamond's engine hummed.

"I need time to think about it."

"Fine." I couldn't fight the smile that spread across my face. She was interested, just like I knew she would be. With her on the job, we'd be rich in no time.

"Will I be expected to put my pound of flesh in to get information from the management or anyone else?"

"Pound of flesh? You mean fuck them?"

"Yes."

I gripped the handles hard until white showed around my knuckles. "I'd rather you not."

"Alright." She sighed. "I'll give you my answer tomorrow night. I've never worked with anybody else before. I'm not sure if I can even trust you or your brothers."

"Have we hurt you in anyway?"

"You shot, kidnapped, and chained me."

"Well, besides that."

"I need time."

"Okay."

My bike lit up with white lights outlining the propellers under the frame. Diamond purred as we rose into the air. And with that purr, I knew the hump Nix sat on emitted sensual vibrations between her thighs. She stirred and scooted back into my very hard dick. But unlike most females, she didn't inch away, instead she arched into my chest and groaned.

"How are you doing so far?" I ached to be inside her, craved to slip my hands around to her breasts and tease those erect nipples.

"I'm doing . . . fine." She rolled her hips so slow, I wasn't sure if it was to rub her ass against me or to ground that sweet pussy onto the vibrating metal.

"Please," I whispered and brushed my lips against her ear, smelling the jasmine and rose fragrance on her skin. "Please let me know if you need anything."

"I'm pretty sure the ride home will be enough." She slid up a little, massaging herself into my bike, and then she slipped back down into me. The cushion of that succulent behind made me falter for a second.

I bet her panties and jeans are soaking wet. I'd give my arm and both of my eyes to feel that moist flesh on my fingertips.

"I'm here if you need anything." I twisted the handles back to rev up the engine.

"I'm good."

Tease.

We lifted higher and hovered over my apartment building. The disappearing sun rested on the silhouette of Turbine city, painting the sky with layers of gold and darkening lavender. I switched on my signal light to notify the aerials speeding by that I would join them. Many gave me a wider berth as they zoomed by pumping the air with music. I revved the engine some more. Tremors waved through the whole bike.

"Epic," she moaned.

"Yes, Nixie baby?" I pressed my hungry dick against her. "What can I do for you?"

Her body trembled under me, but I wouldn't place my hands on her unless she asked. At least I would try my best to control myself.

She cleared her throat. "I'd like some music, please. You know of any good radio stations on this side of earth?"

"That's it?"

"Yes."

I eased into traffic and switched on the radio, pissed and aggravated.

"Could you maybe turn it up louder?" She ground into the hump. I almost bit my tongue off as I gritted my teeth.

She's going to get off while I take her to her room? Is this an invitation or should I just enjoy the ride?

The volume rose. Some idiot sang out about a galaxy love with no limits. I had no idea what else he said as Nix rocked into the bike and me. Her loud moans climbed high above the notes. Young guys in their aerial crafts looked our way with hungry expressions as she humped. Mothers covered their kids' eyes. Fathers nearly crashed into other vehicles as they ogled her hips.

The ride was unbearable. I forced myself to focus on the scenery around me. We'd left my area of North America, soared over the North Atlantic Ocean, and headed for the continent of Africa, where my brothers and I had found Nix in her cheap hotel in the country of Kenya. I hated flying over Africa. Clouds of fumes and gray smoke hovered over the space. Scents of decay and rotten garbage saturated the air. Mountains of landfills expanded throughout the continent and could be seen miles upon miles ahead. Ever since President Templeton signed the agreement ten years before with the Duchess of Light for Africa to serve as the location of all the galaxy's trash, no one but the most downtrodden people lived on the continent.

Nixie stopped rocking as we came closer. No doubt the smell and view had ruined her sensual fun. I gazed down. Crows nested on the points of the landfills. From high up even the rats seemed huge. They looked as big as Turtle. Brown fur covered their fat bodies. I swerved around hover dumpster trucks that lowered into the atmosphere at quick speeds. Their bottoms slid open. Pounds of junk dropped out of the ships and rained down into the landfills.

I lifted us higher, pointing us toward the clouds and away from the filth. The wind transformed from an unpleasant odor to fresh air within seconds. I revved the engine some more, sending strong vibrations to Nix's soft spot between her thighs.

"Epic," Nix moaned.

"Yes, Nixie baby?"

"N-nothing." She returned to rubbing and my dick ached at the view of her sexy body moving around and around on the hump.

"Please let me know if I can do anything."

She said nothing, just moaned more.

And there I sat the whole twenty-minute journey from the northern hemisphere to the south, battling with myself not to wrench my dick out of my jeans, rip a hole in hers, and shove into Nix hard, fucking her nonstop, until that hot pussy gripped my cock with no mercy and dripped down so much cream that I exploded and marked that body as mine.

She's too dangerous.

CHAPTER 6
PHOENIX

I couldn't help the moans that escaped from my lips as Epic's little toy hummed between my legs like a gi-normous vibrator. I definitely was discovering that I had a newfound appreciation for bikes, his in particular. If he was hoping his bike would serve as foreplay and seduction rolled into one, I had news for him. That boat had already sailed. He had his opportunity earlier in the room when I'd let him kiss me and he had walked away.

Maybe he thought he was being noble, but his rejection was like a kick to the gut. I knew his type. He wanted me on his terms, and that was a game I refused to play. It was my way or nothing. Besides, if I did decide to work with him and his brothers, then I wasn't about to mix business with pleasure.

Hot desire burned a path from between my thighs and uncoiled throughout my body. My arousal soaked my panties and probably seeped through my pants, I was so turned on. Licking my lips and arching my back into Epic, I rocked my ass into his hard cock, relishing in its thickness and the fact that it had to be driving him crazy. He whimpered behind me, or maybe it was just my imagination. The need seared into a hunger so strong I rubbed my swollen pussy up and down the hump, clutching at his thighs for support.

"Yes, baby. Right there." I was so close and I didn't care if he knew it. I rolled my hips with abandon, not caring who else knew that I was about to get off either. Apparently, Epic had wanted a show, and I was more than happy to give it to him. "Aaaah . . . Epic . . . go . . . faster."

I grinned as his cock pulsed against my ass and his knuckles gripped the handlebars tighter. "Damn, Nixie baby. You sure you don't need anything from me?"

I smiled, glad he couldn't see my face from his position. If he did, he would have pulled over and taken me right there. "Just keep doing what you're doing."

"I'm not doing anything." Frustration coated his words.

I had to bite my cheek to keep from laughing. "Sure you are, lover boy."

Despite his annoyance at me for being such a big tease, his bike began to pick up speed and I no longer could concentrate on well . . . teasing him anymore. I just wanted to get off.

"Mmmm—aaaaahhh!" I heard myself make some kind of incoherent moan as I pushed myself into the vibrating hump on Epic's bike. "Touch me, Epic. Right now."

One of his hands left the bike and splayed across my stomach. It only stayed there for a moment as I continued to gyrate. His touch drove me to new levels of passion. Twisting my head his way, I leaned back into him, burying half my face against his chest so I could get a good whiff of his enticing spicy scent. Epic's large hand came to rest lightly over my right breast. His body tensed around me and waited for my reaction. Loud moans fled from my lips. He gently squeezed once before pinching my nipple through my thin shirt. *Damn you.* I didn't last much longer after that. I cried out as my thighs quivered. My orgasm exploded through me. Pleasure spasmed in every cell. My body shook with its loss of control.

"Epic," I moaned as little aftershocks racked my body. "I need to get off this thing."

I could feel my body already building toward another release. God, maybe his bike was foreplay and seduction all rolled into one. Between the vibrating hump I was again grinding myself against and the rock-solid cock at my back . . . shit. If Epic wanted to fuck me right here, right now, I'd let him.

"We're here, Nixie baby." Epic's sounded out of breath, like he'd just been running. A small part of me thrilled that I affected him that way.

"Oh. We're here?" I wasn't sure if I was disappointed or not. We came to a stop and Epic only let the bike idle for a moment before turning it off. "Damn, I already knew diamonds were a girl's best friend, but your bike puts a whole new meaning to that phrase. You chose the name wisely." I chuckled to myself and climbed off Diamond, noting that Epic hadn't said anything since turning the bike off, nor had he moved. A bulge was evident in the middle of his pants.

"Well, you coming in, or what?" I asked without looking at him and walked off with shaky legs toward my dark and dingy motel room.

"Yeah" was all he said. He was off his bike and crowding in behind me before I could blink.

Once inside my motel room with the door shut securely behind us, I turned to face Epic. He stood still as a statue just inside the door, almost as if he were unsure of what to do. But that was okay. I liked being in control.

"Come here, lover boy." I curled my fingers invitingly. He swallowed and stepped toward me, his eyes turning a burnt-sienna color. I was fast learning that meant he was turned on . . . very much so.

Epic stopped right in front of me. His gaze raked over the length of my body with heat. He reached out to grab me with his huge hands. Stepping back, I smiled up at him. "I'm not going to let you fuck me."

His succulent lips immediately dipped into a frown. "Then why in the damn darkness did you invite me in?"

"You missed your chance to get into my pants when you left me in those chains."

"You did shoot me twice. I had a reason to put you in those chains until I could talk to you—"

I interrupted him. "I want to thank you for my little ride home. It was very enjoyable. Satisfying, to be exact."

I dropped to my knees before he could react and unzipped his pants. His large cock sprang free, a bead of moisture on the tip already waiting for me. I snaked my tongue out to taste it. *Mmmm . . . delicious. I knew he would taste divine.*

He snapped a picture of my mouth gliding down his cock with reverence.

I slid my mouth off. "I didn't give you permission to take that."

"Trust me. Only I will see it," he assured me before I said anything else. "I won't transfer it to a computer and send it off to anyone."

I guided my tongue up and down his length, pausing to say, "If I see it somewhere in cyber space, then you're dead."

"Yes, ma'am." He bit his lip as all of his attention followed my tongue.

"I love the way you taste." I sucked on the head. The point swelled up within my mouth.

Epic groaned and fisted his hands in my hair as he rocked his hips forward, silently begging me to take him deeper. "Please, Nixie."

I reached up and placed my hands on his hips to stop him from trying to take control. Not many women realized it, but the smart ones knew that a woman could dominate a man from her knees using only her tongue and mouth. The idea of dominating an Alpha male like Epic . . . *oh yeah . . .* that just did all kinds of things to my insides.

"Nixie, baby," Epic groaned in frustration. "Please. Suck on it for me, baby."

I leaned back. His hard cock slipped from my mouth. I licked the edges around the tip. "You want to put in my mouth?"

"Fuck, yes!" His hands combed through my hair. His legs trembled before me. "I'll do anything you desire, Nixie."

Yep, I have him right where I want him . . . at my mercy.

I sucked him between my lips and took his hard length all the way back into my throat. It filled my mouth. My cheeks strained a little. Tilting back, I slowly pulled it out and ran my tongue up underneath the head, and flicked him there. With my other hand I cupped his soft balls and teased them with my fingertips.

"God, you're good, Nixie baby. That's right."

I sucked him back into me, balls deep. His knees buckled as I hummed. "Duchess help me! I can't stand while you do this."

I chuckled with his cock still pushed deep into my throat and walked him backward while on my knees, until his back hit the wall. *There, that should support him.* And then I went to work—tugging with my mouth, licking, and lapping at him with wet strokes. And when he cried out with desire, I knew he was close. I then sucked on just the head.

"Fuck!" He banged the wall behind him and pounded into my mouth.

With me working him, he only lasted a few minutes, but I knew that wasn't a statement about his stamina. I was just that good. Hot liquid spurted into my throat. He wound his hips back and forth, giving it all to me. When he finished, I swallowed down every last drop of his delicious cum. He slumped down to the ground as if drained of energy. His pants rested at his ankles. I rose and took a mental picture of him, wishing I had artificial eyes like him to take real pictures to look back later on the memory.

The dirty motel wall supported all six-foot-whatever of his solid muscle. His hands hung limply at his sides. His head tilted back with his full lips parted slightly and his eyes were firmly shut. His semi-hard dick glistened with my saliva. I liked what I saw, and a small part of me craved to keep him for a little while longer.

But no, it isn't meant to be.

I learned a long time ago that a man like Epic couldn't be trusted in the long run. He would one day yearn to control me—own me—and I wasn't the type of woman who would let either happen to her. I was almost owned once, and it had nearly killed me, but instead it ended up killing him. I shook my head. I didn't need to think about Teddy now or ever.

"Time for you to leave," I stated with no emotion.

Epic's eyes snapped open with surprise. "What do you mean 'time to leave'?"

"What were you expecting? For me to want to cuddle with you afterward?"

"Maybe not cuddle, but—"

"What? Dinner and a movie? Or maybe you figured you'd talk to me for an hour or so and then fuck me on that crappy bed over there?" I quirked an eyebrow at him. "In case you haven't noticed, I'm not really that type of girl."

"Wow. Whoever it was did a real number on you."

"No one did a number on me."

"Someone hurt you so bad you won't give yourself a chance to get to know me."

"What?" *Am I that transparent?*

"You sucked my dick and then tried to kick me out before I could even say thank you or yes, ask you if you wanted to do something or grab something to eat."

"I'm not hungry and I don't do movies."

"That's not the point."

"Save it for someone who wants to listen."

"Then fine, never mind," Epic muttered under his breath. "None of my business anyway. I guess I should at least say thanks or something."

"The pleasure was all mine. Maybe you'll earn another session in the future."

He ran his fingers through his hair and rose, yanking his pants up. He stuffed himself back in his jeans and zipped up. "You're crazy and pure trouble."

"Yeah, but the good kind of trouble."

"I haven't decided that part yet." Epic studied my face, making me grow uncomfortable under his scrutiny. His eyes glowed white and I wondered what that emotion meant. "You're really an amazing woman. From the moment you stole from me, you've had me second guessing every step I make, while my dick is hard for you."

"Goodnight, Epic. I'll let you know about the job tomorrow evening, maybe," I said, trying to hurry along his departure. I couldn't deal with him being in my room any longer, I might do something stupid, like ask him to cuddle or something. Of course after I fucked his brains out . . . probably several times.

He turned to face the door and then glanced over his shoulder at me. "Why the tattoo, the whole phoenix flying out of the fire?"

"Why?"

"I had a dream about it."

I grinned.

"Don't get crazy. The dream wasn't all about you."

I frowned and then forced my face into a neutral mask.

"The dream dealt with my dad. He recently passed away, but at the end a Phoenix rose out of the fire. Why did you get that tattoo?"

Oh, he wanted to know about my tattoo. Most did, and I didn't have a problem sharing its meaning. I'd gotten it as a statement, after all. "Sometimes when a girl is young and stupid, she makes mistakes, and pretty big ones at that. Me—I fucked up something big."

Teddy's face flashed in front of me and I pushed it away.

"Who was it?" Epic asked.

"That's not your concern. I got it to remind me that no matter what, I'll always rise from the ashes. No one will ever keep me down. No one." I practically growled the last part, my emotions taking control of me for a moment.

"I understand that, but not all men are the same." Epic's forehead creased in the middle with worry. "You should remember that."

I gave him a sickening sweet smile. "Oh, how sweet. Are you offering to be the one who opens my eyes up to how great men can be? And maybe you even really believe you're the guy for the job, but things would change. Eventually you'd want to control me, own me, and break me. And it would drive you insane when you couldn't. It would end badly for everyone." I shook my head to rattle some sense into myself. "It's best if we have a business relationship only."

"You call what just happened between us business?" He took a step my way.

"What else could it be? We don't even know each other." I narrowed my eyes at him.

Did I make a mistake? Is he the type that thinks just because we shared a few bodily fluids that he has some kind of claim on me?

"So what was it then?"

"That was just a thank you, like I said. It meant nothing."

Epic stared at me as if at a loss for words, his nostrils flaring with anger.

"Okay. So I'll let you know about the job." I waved at him. "Bye bye now."

Epic opened the door, stalked through, and slammed it behind him without another word. I was going to have to give some serious thought to whether or not working with him was a good idea. I might have already complicated things beyond repair. But, fuck, I needed out of this shit hole and off this planet for good. I had enough money to move to a better room now, but I didn't want to waste it in case I decided I was going to continue on with my original plan and not work with Epic and his brothers.

Fuck, that man is trouble.

CHAPTER 7
EPIC

She's not coming. Fuck her.

I snorted some quake in the transport bathroom. The cold powder dusted my nostril, blasted up my nasal cavity, and entered my bloodstream with a rush of speed and dominance. Next came the smell of sugar mixed with vanilla and butter, then that numb sensation, the reason why I preferred the drug out of all the others. My body deadened to nothing—no feeling or emotions, no worries or insecurities. A soothing fog twirled around me. *Deadness and Mom's cookies.* I closed my eyes and leaned back against the wall.

"Epic, you done? I got to potty." One of my little brothers pounded at the door.

"There's another one down the aisle."

"I gotta go b-bad."

I can't even get peace in the bathroom.

"Okay. Hold on. I'm coming out." I checked the sink.

No trace of the yellow powder on any of the chrome surface. My head spun. I swayed and bumped into the metal wall. It should have hurt, but quake swam in my system. No pain would come for hours. I put on my sunglasses. Since they were artificial, my eyes never turned red after using, but I hated the worried glances from Mimi and the upset glares from Shade and Toy. Somehow they knew I was doing something, but they didn't know what or how. But paranoia always pulsed through my veins when they glanced my way.

"Here you go." Opening the door, I stepped out of the bathroom.

"T-thanks, Epic." Randy raced in, clutching his crotch with a strained expression on his face.

The transport to planet Trinity was a huge vehicle that could hold two hundred and fifty people and was divided into twenty-four large, closed-off sections labeled in the Greek alphabet, from alpha to omega. We were in section omega.

My family sat in their seats, strapped in with double seatbelts that wrapped around their chest and waist. Shade and Toy hung out in seats behind the triplets. The guys were the last line of defense if any of the kids decided to sneak out of our section of the transport and mingle, or in other words, draw kiddie art on the slick tan walls, yank strangers' hair, steal more cookies off the dessert tray, and overall discover some way to destroy the huge machine and our trip as much as possible.

"Everybody okay?" I headed down the blue-carpeted aisle to my seat.

"We are," the triplets sang in unison.

On my left, Mimi read a picture book screen to my baby sister, Chloe. She was three years old. Mom carried and birthed her, then afterward, became sick. I'd quit my gig as lead singer with the band Chameleon and nursed mom for two years. At the end of the second year, she'd died in my arms, and Chameleon topped the galaxy music charts with their new singer. I had no regrets of spending those years with my mom. I learned more about her and got to say goodbye on my own terms, but when the bills piled up, I dreamed about what I could've done for my family if I'd stayed with Chameleon.

"Good morning," the pilot said over the speakers. "We'll be departing shortly."

She's not coming.

I glanced over at Nix's empty seat as I sat down in the one right next to it. After her interesting and pleasurable thank you, I'd rode home feeling like she'd blown my mind as well as my dick.

She was no-nonsense. Other women would've lain on their back, opened their legs, and let me do anything I pleased. Next would've came hugging, kissing, listening to their problems, and then the awkward moment where I ease out of there with no promise of a repeat session. Nix had given me a thanks-for-the-ride-bub blow job and sent me on my way. I returned to her hotel room the next day with flowers and she was gone.

The problem with her having a detailed ink tattoo like that is that men recognized and remembered her wherever she went. In fact, that was why we'd found her so easily the night she stole our money. We had cousins who were covered in electric-wired ink from their ankles to their necks. They existed deep within the tattooing community and knew all things related to the art on the planet. They'd given us a list of all tattoo parlors that still used ink.

The first one we visited had an artist in there that hadn't done the fire and bird but who'd seen Nix before and carried on a conversation with her. He'd been in awe of her ink and told us she lived deep in the core of Underside. Once we arrived in Underside, it cost a few dollars for bums to point us in the right direction.

So two days ago, it took me only an hour to find her new room. I rode through the area and asked around for the sexy, dark-haired girl with a phoenix inked on her back. Some loser sent me to a luxury hotel on the edge of the city. When I walked in the lobby, I caught her fragrance—jasmine and roses. I'd just missed her, the receptionist explained, so I left Nix a message, the flowers, and a transport ticket to Trinity. She'd never called or left a message at the apartment.

And she didn't show up here. She could have at least called.

I shut my eyes and eased into my seat, shoving the image of Nix on her knees out of my mind. *That mouth. Don't think about that soft, moist suctioning.* I stirred in my seat. *Her blow jobs should be illegal on several planets—maybe all of them.*

"Please remain seated." The female voice sounded from the ceiling. "Takeoff will begin in twenty seconds."

And Nix isn't here.

I'd have to change the plan, but it wouldn't be a big deal. I'd only added her in at the last minute. The problem for me would be the damn thoughts about her that had filled my mind for the last few days. I realized we couldn't be more than whatever the hell we were, but I yearned to be it. I daydreamed about the few moments on Trinity when we could tour the planet, dance at any of the fun spots known for good music, and together we'd plan the hit with precision. She had a brain in that gorgeous head. I desired to be inside of it and so much more.

"Twenty." The countdown began.

"Nineteen."

The floor trembled under my feet. The plastic drapes lowered over the windows and darkened the cabin.

"Eighteen."

I plugged my ears with music and switched to the electric heat category. It was the only genre of music I preferred. The music swam into my ears, drenched with that dark, edgy groove and sweltering bass, one ripped so hard I could hear it in my heart and in the rhythm of my pulse. Almost as if the music stopped, I would die within the silence.

"You ripped me open until I was raw with you." The singer's deep voice flowed on the edge of erotic and menace. *"And then you laughed and savored my pain from you."*

Someone tapped my arm. I quickly opened my eyes in anticipation, hoping it was Nix, but it wasn't. Just a huge robot dressed in shining blue metal that was as wide as a door. Its middle looked like a four-foot box. The head twisted my way as the transport took off.

I yanked out my head phones and pulled off my sunglasses. "Yeah?"

"Compliments of Ms. Phoenix, sir." The robot's boxed center slid open to reveal three large champagne bottles on a tray with a glass filled with slabs of roasted meat over rice, a bowl of chocolate cookies, and pitchers of ice-cold milk. "I was ordered to go to this area and provide section omega with these items."

"All of this is for me?" I sat up in the seat.

"No, sir." The tray pushed out toward me. Words lit up around its eyes as if the machine were reading the message. I heard cheers from the kids and knew they'd spotted the cookies.

"Who did Ms. Phoenix say these were for?" I asked.

Several gleaming violet wires swirled out of his sides, captured one bottle, and handed it to me. "It is all for section omega. The three bottles of champagne were to be delivered to a Mr. Epic Failure, Mr. Beaded Monstrosity, and Mr. Toy Chains. The rest were for the family of cretins."

A grumble boomed from the back. I figured it was Shade since Toy had exploded with laughter. Mimi gestured for the robot to come to her. I was sure she'd hold on to the cookies and milk and dole them out a little at a time in an effort to keep the kids being good for their sweet prize.

"Was there a message?" I balanced on the edge of joy that Nix had thought of us and fear that the food was an apology to say she wasn't coming.

"Yes, sir." The robot rolled over to my sister, but its head remained facing me. "Ms. Phoenix said that she is on the transport and will meet you at the baggage area when the craft lands."

Fuck that. I want to see her now.

"And where is she?" I undid my seatbelts and rose.

"All humans are supposed to remain seated during launch and until the captain states otherwise."

"I have an emergency."

Red lights glowed on the top of its head. "All humans are supposed to remain seated during launch and until the captain states otherwise."

"I'll be back."

The robot's head spun a few times and then it gave up on me and handed over the cookies to Mimi. *If it was a human transport stewardess, my butt would have been shoved back into the seat. There is definitely a good side to machines.* Toy grabbed the plates and utensils. Frowning, Shade reached for the meat and rice.

"We're not hungry for rice. We want dessert." The triplets bounced in their seat in perfect unison. "Cookies! Cookies!"

"Enough! Dinner first and if you're good, then sweets," I roared. They sank into their seats. I turned to the robot. "Where is Ms. Phoenix?"

"I do not know, sir." The robot continued down the aisle.

"Can you provide any other information?"

"This meal was billed to a Mr. Doug McIntyre in section alpha. Good day, sir."

Alpha? She's in first class and this McIntyre must be her first whale to Trinity.

Jealousy merged with my temper and boiled in my gut. It was sweet that she'd gotten the food for us. Transport food was pricey and cost three times a regular meal. With the price of the tickets, fee for moving furniture, and all of the other expenses incurred, all I could get the kids were a couple of crackers and bottles of water. We were on a strict budget once we hit Trinity. I battled with myself to relax, sit back in my seat, and just take the food.

But then images of a strange man sucking on Nix's breast danced in my head. *Who is this McIntyre guy and why did he pay for her? Did she suck him off too?* I shook away that thought. It wasn't my business, but I couldn't get the questions out of my mind. Instead, I followed my path of rage.

"Where you going, man?" Shade raised his black eyebrows.

"To say thank you."

"Just thank you?"

"Maybe," I said through clenched teeth.

"You think that is a smart move?"

"Why wouldn't it be?"

He waved me away and started to spoon food onto plates. "It's probably not a good idea to piss her off for being nice, just because you're jealous."

"I'm not jealous."

I would just love to say thank you to Mr. McIntyre with my fist and perhaps a foot deep within the crevices of his ass.

"I'll be right back." I stormed out of our section and stomped toward alpha, opening and closing doors to get to each section, as well as passing many compartment passengers who were pissed off I was walking through their area.

I arrived in alpha in no time. Nix's laughter hit me first. It came out smooth and melodic, like a song. The fragrance of jasmine and roses fluttered toward me next. I centered my attention toward the direction and trapped her in my view.

Her usual straight midnight hair now hung in a waved pattern. An artistic touch of makeup decorated her olive skin, not too much to give her a cheap appearance, but enough to imprison any man that gazed her way. And she'd jailed them all. Every man ogled her, from young to old, single or taken. She wore an olive-green leather strapless corset over a matching long-sleeve blouse, which topped a long green-and-black brocade skirt.

It was the rich lady's new style on Trinity. They set the fashion trends, and the style now was modesty through yards of expensive fabric in a modern twist to nineteenth century dress. Mimi had blasted my ear all about it the night before as she poured through fashion magazines on the planet. I'd planned on buying Mimi several of these dresses and loved the idea of covering her up. But now I wasn't sure if the covering up part was a simple solution for my sister's new body, because just one glance at Nix's dress incited a craving to rip that silk and leather, break away that skirt, and devour her center.

She giggled again and then turned my way as if she'd felt someone new looking at her. The smile plastered her face, but worry crinkled around the edges.

"Brother! You've come to visit me." She motioned me over and turned to a slim brown man with a gray mustache that curled up at the edges. "I told you my family is so protective of me. He's probably here to check on me."

So now I'm her brother? No wonder this dumb guy paid. He probably thought the food was for family.

"Of course. That is what a proper brother should do." The man patted her arm and kept his gaze on the spill of olive bosom that peeked from the corset since Nix seemed to have forgotten to button up her blouse.

"*Brother* dear," Nix stressed the word, "don't just stand there. Come here."

Fine. I'll play your game.

"Dear sister, you look lovely, as usual. Is this your fishing outfit or have you guaranteed your catch for today?" I clapped and spoke in a high voice. She cringed, and I laughed boldly.

The poor guy, lost in her bosom, nodded his head as if he were listening to the conversation, but I knew what was in his mind as his slithering tongue dapped at a bead of sweat near his mustache.

"My brother considers himself a comedian." She moved a little and the tops of her breasts jiggled with the movement. I doubted it was innocent or a coincidence as she winked at me. "I'm not a fan of fishing. I much prefer to have my meals come to me willingly."

"I bet you do." I got up right next to them, leaned toward Mr. Lip-Licking McIntyre, and in a blur, wrapped my hand around his neck. "Make sure that tongue remains in your mouth and those hands stay to the side the whole trip. My nose is full of enhanced sensors. I smell you on my . . . sister and I spend my first day in glorious Trinity wiring you to an opened electric socket with your intestines."

"Let him go. Now, dammit." Nix beat against my arm.

I looked at her and tightened my grip on his neck. "Let go of who?"

The poor guy struggled to breath. His brown skin darkened. He pushed at my fingers with his hands. The people around us turned away, no doubt pressing an emergency button or signaling for robotic security.

"Epic, stop," Nix snarled.

I released him and backed up. "Sorry."

McIntyre bobbed his head. "No. No. That's okay."

"It's just when I think of my sister's virginity being taken, I worry." I shrugged.

The fool cleared his throat and massaged his neck. "Of course. I understand."

Nix jumped up and smoothed down the silk material with her hands. "We need to talk, brother dearest."

"Where?"

"Bathroom." She marched off to the end of her aisle. The green leather shined in the transport's light as it trailed behind her. Even pissed off and rushing away, she hypnotized me.

"And what are we going to talk about, dear sister?" I called after her as I strolled her way.

She glared at me, yanked open the door, and hurried in.

I stifled a chuckle and covered my dick with my hands, knowing that would probably be the first thing she'd strike. It took me long enough, but I was slowly unfolding this puzzle of a woman.

First rule: if you piss her off, then cover your equipment.

CHAPTER 8
PHOENIX

I stared up into Epic's chiseled face as I pulled the door shut behind us in the tiny transport bathroom. He looked slightly nervous, like I might hit him or something. The thought made me smile. I jerked my arm suddenly and laughed out loud when his large hands cupped his crotch protectively as he flinched away from me.

"What's so funny?" Epic grumbled while eyeing me warily.

"I'm not going to hit you." I bit my lip and smirked. "It's no fun when you're prepared for it."

Epic grimaced as my words sank in. "You're one sadistic bitch."

"I've been called worse." I frowned. "What was that about out there?"

"Just a brother taking care of his sister." He spit the words out like they disgusted him.

"Don't do that again." I waved my hand toward the door.

K.D. PENN

"I won't promise you that I won't. In fact, I probably will do it every time I see a piece-of-crap guy near you."

"Why? We're just friends." An exasperated breath left my lips. I had a sinking feeling I already knew. My little intimate thank you to him the other day had him feeling possessive. Maybe I should have cuddled him. Nothing like a clingy woman to send a guy like Epic running for the hills. He only wanted me because he couldn't have me. I knew his type. Teddy had been the same way.

Fresh anger rolled off Epic as he glared down at me. "You really going to whore yourself out to the likes of *him*?"

I moved close enough to Epic that we were only separated by a hair's width. I wasn't about to tell him I don't whore myself out. I'm a grade-A first-class tease. When things got too serious, I bounced. "It's none of your business what I do. You have no claim on me. Business is the only type of relationship between us."

"Business?" He spat. "If what you did to me the other day was business, then I don't want you doing business with anyone else."

"You have no claims on me," I hissed before letting a saccharine smile settle on my face. "And besides, that was just a friendly little mouth hug."

Epic's jaw dropped. "A-a mouth hug?" he sputtered, causing me to laugh.

"Yes, a mouth hug. It was a thank you for that wonderful ride home you and Diamond gave me."

"You hug a lot of guys with your mouth?" Epic asked with a scowl.

"It's none of your business what I do with my mouth, or any other part of my body, for that matter." I couldn't resist the urge to press myself against his large frame while running my hands up his muscular arms. "If you stop being an extreme thug trying to control me, then maybe you'll be gifted with another mouth hug."

His body tensed.

"You want another one, don't you?"

"Yes, and I'd rather that sexy mouth not hug anyone else." He glared at me and tugged me toward him so my whole body smoothed against his. I inhaled his cologne and my eyes fluttered shut briefly.

Damn, he smells good.

"We're not together. You don't get to tell me what I do with anyone else."

He slid his hands down the sides of my body. Goosebumps rose wherever he touched. "Then leave this guy alone and just hang with me until the hit is over."

"Two months?"

"Not that long at all." He cupped my ass and groaned.

"It's not in my plan, Epic."

He dipped his head and whispered in my ear, "But it could be." His lips brushed against the lobe. Pleasure blossomed in my chest.

I can't do this.

"No." My eyes snapped open and I pushed away from him.

"What do you mean *no?*" He sucked on the curve of my neck and dove his hands into my corset. His fingers seized a nipple. I slapped his hand away.

"Not going to happen," I stated flatly, even though my nipples pebbled from desire and hardened. "I'm sorry if you got the wrong idea, Epic, but there's nothing but business between us. So stop fucking around and leave me to attend to Mr. McIntyre. Go back with your family, where you belong."

"Oh, that's rich. You actually think you belong with these people? Like you could fit in with them." Anger seeped from every pore of Epic's body, causing his skin to flush.

"I do fit in, in case you haven't noticed. I—"

Epic's hand slammed above my head, causing me to flinch involuntarily. "You don't fit in. They just want to fuck you."

"All men just want to fuck me. That never changes where ever I go." I wasn't clueless. Men were men, no matter their station in life.

Epic's hand slid down the wall and fisted in my hair. "It doesn't have to be that way. I could take care of you."

Arrogant man.

"I don't need you or anyone to take care of me. I can take care of myself." I was seething. How dare he think I needed him or anyone to take care of me.

"Yeah, you were doing so well in that shitty-ass place you were living in." Epic's other hand came to rest on my hip, his fingers pressing into me. I inhaled sharply, resisting the sudden urge to press myself into him. "You don't need someone to take care of you, but you're out there pushing yourself up on some ugly rich guy."

"He's a means to an end and I was doing fine without you. Especially once you provided me with all that money."

"See, I'm already providing for you." Epic's hand slipped from my hip to cup my ass. I wasn't sure why, but I didn't protest when he pulled me back snug against him.

"Is that what you call me ripping you guys off?" I asked breathily.

"Yeah, sure, whatever you want, Nixie baby," Epic rumbled distractedly. "You've been on my mind every moment of these past days. I've been thinking of you and dreaming I'd get a chance to be near you. You think of me, Nixie baby?"

"A little."

"Just a little?" He groaned as I undulated my hot core against his thigh. God, I loved it. His firm muscles tightened against my throbbing center. The hand he had in my hair moved to cup the back of my neck and he brought his forehead down to rest against mine. His other hand began pulling my skirt up, one slow merciless inch at a time.

What is it about this man?

Everything in my mind said no, but everything in my body said yes. Hadn't I learned anything from my relationship with Teddy?

"I think about sitting down and just talking to you and looking into those amazing green eyes of yours."

"Epic," I moaned as his fingers finally slipped along the bare skin of my thigh.

"But most of all, I think about slipping inside of you." He then pulled me roughly to meet his lips. His tongue dove into my mouth to take control and I let him. I reached up and tangled my fingers in his long blond hair, sighing because it was as soft as I had imagined. But something was wrong. A familiar tang washed over my taste buds, one that I could never forget.

No way. Not Epic too.

I ripped myself away from Epic's embrace. "Quake!"

His eyes widened with surprise and his expression confirmed what I already knew to be true. "Why'd you say that word?"

"Because you're a fucking drug addict." *Just like Teddy*! I mentally screamed. *How could I be so blind?*

"No, I'm not an addict I'm just—"

"That's what they all say," I spat at him. "But I can assure you, whether that's your first or thousandth snort, you're already an addict. Quake isn't a social drug. Junkies prefer it most of all because it hooks you at the first snort and never lets go."

"That's not true. I'm no junkie," Epic growled.

I pushed at him, my stomach clenching with disgust. *How could I have let him touch me?* Another Quake addict. "Get out of my way. This was a mistake. I shouldn't have agreed to work with you."

Epic grabbed my arm roughly as I tried to push past him in the small space. "I can stop anytime I want."

I closed my eyes and shook my head, not wanting to look at him. "If you think that, then it's already too late for you."

"No it's not." Epic's grip loosened at my words and I pushed out of the bathroom. I hurried back to my seat beside Mr. McIntyre and hoped Epic wouldn't follow me.

As I sat, Mr. McIntyre looked up at me and frowned. "Problem, my dear?"

"Yes." I pushed down a sob. "My brother, well he…" I leaned forward and whispered in his ear, "I think he's on drugs."

"No." He gasped, wrapping his arm around me as I laid my head on his shoulder. "I'm so sorry. Do you know what kind?"

Oh, I knew exactly what Epic was on, and I knew exactly what quake would do to him too. With each snort, it ate away the user's mind. In a year or less, twisted delusions would swim through his brain. He would need it all the time, every minute of every hour. He wouldn't be able to do anything without it—eat, walk, shit, or sleep. And then the rage would overtake him. Anger merged with delusions would mean that someone would have to handle him before he killed or injured anyone.

Do his brothers know?

"Darling, I'm so sorry." Mr. McIntyre hugged me some more. "What can I do for you? I'd do anything. I know we've only known each other for a day, but I feel a connection between us."

"Me too." *What can he do for me in regards to Epic? Nothing.* But if I was going to play off Epic's erratic behavior to my benefit, I had to not break character. "I-I'm not sure," I stammered. "I can just tell—I've seen it before."

Mr. McIntyre patted my back and slid his hand down much too close to my ass. I stiffened for a moment and then began to sob. My breakdown stopped his roaming hand in its tracks. "I don't know what to do."

"Now, now, I'll take care of everything." He patted me.

I continued to sob even though a small smile played on my face. I tilted my head just in time to see Epic come to stand in my line of vision. He scowled. I narrowed my eyes at him, hoping he wasn't stupid enough to bother me here again. He met my gaze, his jaw clenching, before he turned and stalked back off toward the omega section.

That's right. Take your junkie self back to where you came from. I can only dedicate my heart to one junkie in a lifetime. Anymore and I would crumble into nothing.

Getting involved with Epic was the last thing I needed. Yeah, he was hot, scorchingly so, but him and his brothers were thugs and he was a quake addict. Even though it looked like we'd have a brighter future with this hit, if I hung around with Epic and his quake habit, I'd be broke again before I knew it.

My days of being poor are done.

I'd grown up in a broke family on a dusty planet at the end of the galaxy called Voldun. My ancestors were Italian and the first to leave earth for Voldun once the planet was deemed safe to live on. In those times, babies hadn't been automatically inserted with extra air passages that allowed for survival on other planets with a nonexistent supply of oxygen, at least not enough for humans to live on. Skin graph cells weren't even being injected into newborns, which now is a normal part of the labor procedure. Therefore, my ancestors served as guinea pigs. Many of them died, my mother had said. The few that survived the surgeries lived in pain on Voldun for many years.

Additionally, the Voldunese population wasn't too excited about having a mass of earthlings flooding their planet and bring with them disease. Earthlings could only get the jobs that no else wanted—cave scrubber, metal miner, and service to the lower-class Voldunese.

Things hadn't changed by the time I was born. Poverty lingered throughout childhood, but I always knew I was meant for more. Jewels and fine clothes made me comfortable—at least it did in the secret dreams I had late at night, far away from my father's spying eyes and my mother's disapproving expressions.

My dad and mom were strict, religious fanatics. They prayed to the Duchess of Light once she was re-elected into office as the head of the galaxy. She'd claimed she was immortal and a reincarnation of the Omni goddess, who created stars and life within the universe. I never bought it, even though she'd been the head of the galaxy for over a hundred years. She looked twenty and appeared like she would never die. Rumors spread that she was an android. People caught spreading that message were swiftly killed.

My dad was a Duchess of Light enforcer. He killed with no mercy if people didn't obey her. His relationship with his religion meant everything to him, so much that when he'd discovered me, as a teen, reading a magazine that was forbidden by the Duchess of Light, he beat me to a pulp. My mother stood by as he pounded his closed fists into my face. He kicked my stomach until blood spurted out of my mouth. And still he didn't stop, he yanked me up by my hair and forced me to sing the five hymns of illumination over and over until my throat was raw and my knees buckled under me. When he was satisfied, he threw me back on the ground. My mother stepped to me and relief swept over my body. Surely she would comfort and hold me, wrapping me in a mother's love.

She didn't. Instead, she whispered, "You're a disappointment to us all."

I left that night, hitchhiking from the roof of an abandoned building so that drivers on the aerial highway could see me. My first ride carried me to an abandoned section of Mars and told me that in order to leave, I had to put my mouth on his shriveled dick. That was my first blow job. I hadn't even known what I was doing. Not that the sick pervert cared. The second ride, I met Teddy and figured he was my salvation.

"Let's get you a nice glass of wine," Mr. McIntyre said. "Call me Pappy, by the way."

"No problem." I sniffed and wiped at a few fake tears that lingered.

"Shall we have some lobster brought up too, as well as sang shells from the coast of Longoria?"

I nodded. I'd heard of sang shells. They were supposed to be the most expensive seafood in the universe. I'd never tried it, but now I wanted to, if only to get my mind off Epic.

Epic stood in that bathroom and acted like he wanted to date me. But that could never be. I was meant for bigger and better things than what someone like Epic could offer me. Class wasn't just about money. It was about attitude. Nor did Epic strike me as the brightest crayon in the box. *Not if he's doing drugs.* Some men got brains, and some men got the bodies, very rarely did they receive both. I doubted Epic was hiding some kind of brilliant intellect behind that beautiful face of his. I needed someone who could understand me and accept me for who I really was, not just want me for the way I looked. Clearly Epic wasn't that guy.

Maybe I'd never find him.

CHAPTER 9
EPIC

She says I'm an addict?

I tried to sleep the rest of the trip. My fingers itched for quake. The drug sang to me the whole six-hour flight, whistling a groove that caused me to stir in my seat, moving side to side every few seconds. Nevertheless, I remained in my chair and kept the drug in my pocket. It was like snorting would prove Nix was right, whether she could see me or not, and the last thing I desired was truth escaping from her whale-fishing lips. *Fuck her.* At the end of the trip, I poured the stuff down the commode, flushed it, and then cried with regret for a whole minute because I'd actually thrown it all away.

She's still wrong. I'm not an addict. Right?

Once the transport landed on Trinity, my mind sank in a pit of suffering. My craving for quake rose and rose, higher and higher. The need for the drug severed my senses into a ball of unwanted feelings. Emotions battered my brain. Crazy thoughts exploded inside my head—things I'd left unsaid with Mom, the sad state of my life, and secret insecurities flourished. The possibilities of what my life could have been unwound themselves in my head like an expensive car I got to test drive, but never would own.

In other words, I felt like crap and excused negative energy.

My sunglasses remained on my face, concealing the bad guy from my family, the pitiful sap that quake conquered. Because by the time we approached baggage claim, I could no longer deny Nix's accusations. My body itched. My fingers trembled. My heart pounded in my ears.

I'm an addict.

"Are you okay, man?" Shade loaded our cab with everyone's luggage. The aerial boasted twenty seats. Glass made up the whole cab. I didn't spy any metal or rubber underneath, just a glass body, silver propellers under it, and blue pillow seats inside.

"Epic?" Shade waved his hand in front of my face. "I asked if you were okay."

"Yes. I'm fine." I stood in front of the cab. Everyone else sat in the vehicle, strapped into their seat belts, staring at me. I didn't budge. My shaking hands rested in my pockets. Shade climbed in. I remained outside and kept my eyes closed under my sunglasses.

I just need a minute to get myself together.

My skin prickled in irritation. My bag sat in front of my feet. I couldn't even pick up my own sack. When I tried to lift it, my muscles broke apart as if I had no strength. My fingers shook some more at the thought of running down someone and asking them where the nearest dealer was. Dryness corroded my mouth.

"Epic?" Mimi's voice held concern.

"Epic!" the triplets sang.

The cab driver honked the horn. "What's going on? Is he coming or what?"

"I just need a minute." I opened my eyes. All of my siblings gazed back at me with anxiety. They looked at me like I knew the next steps. *But I don't.* I was supposed to know, but right now I couldn't even think straight. I just wondered where quake would be sold on the planet.

Why did I throw it away? I was fine. I just needed another hit.

"Epic?" Mimi leaned out the window, "what's wrong?"

Get it together. She's scared.

I rubbed the pads of my fingers against each other. My heart raced. Sweat drenched my skin. I opened and closed my mouth as if that would help, but it didn't.

"Toy or Shade, go get Epic's stuff!" Nix walked up to my side, but kept a foot between us. "Are you guys completely oblivious to the fact that the air is messing with his head? He's sick from the transport ride and all of you are just staring around at him like idiots."

"I-I'm . . . fine." *I can't deal with her right now.*

"Be quiet. I know what you are and it isn't fine." She fanned herself with her hand and loudly said, "It's going to take me some time to get used to the oxygen levels here on Trinity. Not all of us are so adaptable. I guess some of us need more time for such things."

She's trying to cover for me.

I stiffened. Embarrassment slid over my skin. I could've sighed, if I had enough focus to think about anything else but quake. The drug rattled my brain.

How did I let my habit get so bad?

"Darling?" Mr. McIntyre appeared with a cart that moved on its own, full of several bags I figured were Nix's. "Did you get the address for where your family is moving to? The sooner we get your stuff there, the faster I can show you around the planet."

Nix hooked her arm around mine. "My brother isn't feeling very well at the moment. The air seems to be getting to him."

Mr. McIntyre winked. "Yes. The air. I understand. Shall we call it a night or should we just get your brother safely home?"

I had several answers for him, ones that dealt with pain and torture, yet I kept my mouth closed. Nix rescued me in a moment of weakness. I wouldn't have her regret it. She wanted to spend time with this guy, so I would step aside.

I'm not even in any shape to be in the way.

"I'm going to need to take care of him tonight, it seems." She tensed against my arm. "We can meet tomorrow. Shade, can you please give Pappy our address?"

Pappy? What kind of first name is Pappy?

"Epic has the address." Shade jumped out.

"*Okaaaay*, and why is he the only one that has it?" she asked.

"He coordinated everything."

Slowly, I dug my hand in my jacket, dropped the paper in his hand, and mumbled, "Here it is."

"See. He had it." Shade gestured to me.

"Seriously, Shade?" she whispered and then scowled at him. "Is Epic the only grown man amongst all of you?"

"I work." Shade shrugged. "And you don't know our situation."

"I know enough. It's truly pathetic that the guy hooked on drugs is the one taking care of everyone," she whispered so the kids wouldn't hear her, yanked his shirt, pulled him our way, and whispered some more, "Can't you see that Epic is hooked on quake? He's drowning right in front of your eyes and you're not doing a damn thing to help him. Help him—help your family. Be a fucking man."

I blew out air. My lips quivered. "It's not like—"

"Just be quiet." She tugged me toward the cab. Her tiny frame yanked me forward as if she were bigger than me. "Give Pappy the damn address, Shade."

Shade mumbled something, but did what he was told. In the end, I believe she scared both of us. Regardless, I climbed inside and eased my way to the back. Once I got to the seats, I just collapsed right there, closing my eyes and sighing.

Nix sat next to me. She clasped her hand onto mine. Warm fingers softened around me. And in that instance, I would've given her anything she desired, just to keep her next to me. It had nothing to do with sex. Her presence just soothed me. Her scent swarmed onto my skin and shoved away the crawling itch of my need for quake. She talked to the triplets about something. I had no idea what she was saying as I leaned my head back into the hard edge of the glass seat and drifted on her voice. I only concentrated on the tone of her words and the way her silky Underside accent slipped out of her lips.

The cab vibrated around us as it moved along.

"Dear Duchess of Light, this planet is so beautiful," Mimi exclaimed. "Thanks so much, Epic."

"I'm glad you like it," I managed to say, but didn't open my eyes.

Loud chatter ensued. They all yapped about whatever they saw outside the window—yellow waterfalls spilling over stark-white mountains, blue grass expanding over unsettled space, crowds of people draped in silk and leather, cruising on personal hover pads that sat under their feet and glided them toward their destination.

I wished I could've taken the time to see and enjoy the views with them, but in that moment all I could do was submerge myself in Nix's scent and hope for my sanity to maintain balance. Noise lifted around us. For some reason all the boisterous conversations comforted me. No one was looking for Epic to take the lead, so I could relax and just be Epic.

Nix pressed her body into me and brushed her lips against my ear. "I want to make sure you don't misconstrue things. My help is still only about business. Don't think it's anything more than what it is."

"I don't." I inhaled her and relished in her closeness. "But thank you. I did need you."

"Yeah, and you still need me."

Sighing, I tightened my grip around her hand as she moved her lips away from my ear. "Maybe. I do, but I think it's probably best if we give each other some space."

"What the fuck happened to you? You seemed fine while you were going all Neanderthal on me in section alpha."

"Well, after I left you, I flushed my tube of quake down the commode to prove to myself that you were wrong. However, it seems you were right."

Silence spread around us for a minute. I wondered what went through her mind.

She probably thinks I'm stupid. And sadly, I knew that she would be right.

"So this is withdrawal?" Her voice sounded shaky.

"Yes." *For now.* "But maybe this isn't the time to try and quit. Maybe I should just go back to—"

"No. That would be disappointing."

I didn't want disappoint her. *Why?* I didn't know, but for some reason, I didn't want to stare at that beautiful face and see disappointment swim behind those irises. Even if I could never have her, I needed her to not see me as undesirable. I longed to be someone she was proud of.

How pitiful is that? I desire her damn approval.

"You need to at least try to quit," she offered. No malice draped those words. She sounded like she cared or maybe that was what I craved to believe, that somewhere within her hard steel exterior there was a woman who gave a damn about whether I died or lived.

"Okay," I muttered. "I'll try and quit."

She snorted. "Seriously . . . you're actually going to give quitting a go? I've seen stronger people than you succumb to quake. It's some hardcore shit."

My mom and dad's faces flashed through my mind. "I've survived a lot. I'm sure I could make it through this."

"When were you planning to do the hit?"

The triplets began singing a song about strawberry-colored dolls with wings. Toy and Shade clapped along. The twins stomped their feet. I couldn't see the cab driver's face, but I'd bet all of my cubes from the future hit he was aggravated.

I leaned into Nix and whispered, "At the end of the week, if everything goes right, we're going to rob the club."

"So you think that you can pull off a major hit on a huge strip club while going through withdrawal from quake at the same time? Someone might be overconfident in themself." Doubt lingered in her tone.

I hated hearing it. "I can do it."

"Not without help."

"I know. I'll talk to Shade and Toy about it."

"No." She pulled off my sunglasses. "I'll help."

Opening my eyes, I raised my head and looked at her. Her gaze froze me, so much emotion radiated from her, but I couldn't get a signal of what she was feeling.

"I'll help you." She exhaled. "I've dealt with something like this before."

"The guy that died?"

She bit her lip. "Yeah."

"Are you going to tell me what happened in that situation?"

"It's none of your business, so no, I'm not going to tell you," she snapped. "Why do you need to know anyway?"

"I'd rather not die from your services." I tossed her a weak smile.

"Then don't fuck with me." She targeted those lovely green eyes on mine.

I shifted my attention to her full lips and then quickly turned away. "Okay. I'll take your help."

She laughed. "Like I'm giving you a choice."

I leaned my head to the side. "Don't I get a choice, Ms. Phoenix?"

"No." She wagged her finger at me. "You put dreams of cubics and the kind of life I want in my little head, and now here I am. You wanted me here, remember? I'm not about to let your addiction to quake fuck up my plans. You won't be using quake during this heist."

"Why not?"

"Because I don't let anyone mess with my money."

I grabbed my sunglasses from her hand and placed them back on my face. "So what's the plan?"

"You continue on with the arrangement for the hit, and I'll make sure your nose remains clean until we're done."

"How will you do that? You're not exactly known for being a sensitive, loving individual."

She grinned. "Just do everything that I tell you and you'll be just fine."

"For some reason, that scares the shit out of me."

"It should."

CHAPTER 10
PHOENIX

How the fuck did I get myself into this situation?

I swore I'd never deal with another addict again. And here I was, with Epic, in a hotel room . . . alone. I mean . . . what the fuck?

"Motherfucker!" I swore out loud, causing Epic's massive sweat-slicked form to groan. He lay face down, spread across the massive king-sized bed. And I'd spent some of my hard-earned money to get us here. Mine . . . not his.

It'd become quite evident I wasn't going to be able to help Epic through his withdrawal with his family around and manage to keep it a secret from his younger brothers and sisters. I wasn't really sure why I cared if they found out. Epic meant nothing more than a big paycheck and a ticket to a new life for me. And yet I'd paid for this stupid high-end room at the last minute to get him away from his family. You would have thought Shade and Toy would have offered to help, but no. They were too busy being the selfish brats I'd accused them of being. I should have just gone with Pappy and forgotten about it all.

"Nix?" Epic's strained voice rasped.

As if my body had a will of its own, I found myself sitting next to Epic's large form. I smoothed his damp hair back from the side of his face. His eyes fluttered open but didn't seem to be able to focus.

"Nix?"

"I'm right here, Epic. Did you need something?" *Goddammit! I just need to let him sweat this out, literally. Why the hell am I being so sweet to him?*

"This is useless. I c-can't. Just get me some quake." His eyes slid back shut as if he were ashamed. And damn well he should be.

"No. I'm not getting you any quake. You're detoxing whether you like it or not." I clenched my teeth together so hard my jaw started to ache.

"Nixie baby, p-please."

My hand fisted in his hair and I angrily yanked his head back. He screeched. His eyes flew open as he grimaced at me.

"Don't you dare beg me for drugs," I hissed. "You won't like my reaction."

"Okay. Okay." A pathetic smile tugged at his lips. "I kind of like you being rough with me. Would I get more of that if I beg?"

Now he's a comedian? I released his head abruptly and his face dropped to the pillow.

"Men." I grumbled under my breath as I stood. All of them were completely incorrigible.

"Nixie, d-don't go," Epic started again. "Are you l-leaving me?"

"No!" I rubbed my face with both my hands. "Unfortunately, I'm not going anywhere until you're good enough to get up and walk without begging for quake."

A quiet descended over the room for a while. For a few seconds, I believed he might have fallen asleep and was thankful he'd be getting some rest.

"Will you hold me?" Epic's voice dipped down low with his vulnerability. My heart broke just a little for him. I was only human after all.

"Yeah. I'll hold you," I mumbled. "Just let me change into something that I won't mind getting ruined by sweat."

"I won't mind if you get naked." Epic grinned at me, but the happy expression dropped and that sad, embarrassed look he'd been wearing most of the day returned.

I shook my head and chuckled, trying to lighten the mood. "Yeah, I'm sure you would like me naked."

I grabbed my bag and headed into the bathroom. I quickly changed out of my travel clothes and slipped into matching green cotton shorts and a tank top. The soft fabric hugged my curves and comforted me. I slowly crept back into the hotel room and made my way to the bed. I stared down at Epic. He lay still. I wondered if he had finally fallen asleep.

His eyes were closed and his breathing was even. He had kicked off the sheets to expose his boxer-only-clad behind. I couldn't help but take the opportunity to admire him. He had the classic V-shape to his body—large defined back and shoulders that tapered down to a narrow waist. His long, silky blond hair was dampened with sweat, but it still made me itch to run my fingers through it. His chiseled face was masculine and yet his lips were full and succulent, begging to be kissed. He wore a silver chain with a locket shaped like a heart. I wondered whose picture was inside it. Irrational jealousy spiked through my system.

Yeah, I need to stop thinking about him in any other way than business. He's a means to an end, and that's it.

"Nixie baby," Epic mumbled, somehow sensing my presence without opening his eyes, "I thought you were going to let me hold you."

I frowned. "You asked me to hold you."

"We can hold each other."

His words made something in my heart stir, and it pissed me off. "I've changed my mind. No one's holding anyone. Just try and get some sleep."

"*Pleeeaase,*" he slurred. "I need you to . . . Fuck. I don't know. I-I just need you."

I sighed, knowing I would give in. He was kind of pathetic at the moment.

"Fine." I snapped.

I slid into bed next to him and he immediately curled himself around me, pushing his face into my neck and inhaling. The contact was electric. Even with him trying to recover from quake, his body still radiated a predatory sexuality my body couldn't ignore. He wrapped his arms around my middle and possessively slung one of his muscled legs over my tinier ones. I felt safe for the first time in years and had no idea why. It wasn't like he could jump up, as sick as he was from withdrawal, and protect my honor. But, for some weird reason, as my body lay next to him, the sensation of protection folded over me like a blanket.

"Goodnight, Epic."

He sighed in contentment and his breathing began to even out. Against my will, my fingers stroked his hair. The silky strands slipped underneath my fingertips and smelled of bubble gum. *He must have washed his hair with one of his sisters' shampoo.* I chuckled a little to myself, careful not to wake him. My fingers sank into his hair and remained until I joined him in sleep.

Hours later, I awoke with a start, my heart thundering in my chest because I couldn't move my arms. Someone held me. He encased me in muscle and was too huge to move. I couldn't get free.

"No!" I screamed as I flailed in an effort to free myself. "Teddy, no!"

Whatever was constricting my movements was suddenly gone and someone shook me. "Nix—Nixie baby—it's me—Epic."

I blinked away my confusion and focused on Epic's face. Worried lines edged the corners of his eyes as they flickered between blue and black, belaying his concern and pity.

I gritted my teeth. "Let me go. I don't like feeling constricted."

"I'm sorry." Epic sat up and stared me as I studied him. His skin appeared less pale. His hands didn't shake. Clearly he was feeling better. Not good, but better. Quitting quake wasn't going to be that easy, but the initial physical withdrawal was over. The rest would be up to him—or, really, me.

"What happened? What were you dreaming about?"

"You're feeling better, I see," I stated trying to change the subject.

"Yes. I am." He sighed. "You yelled out *Teddy*. Is that the guy that hurt you?"

"He can't hurt me anymore. Let's talk about something else."

"What did he do to you?" Epic asked, not allowing me to drop it.

"That's none of your business." I wasn't going to just drop all my baggage on someone who wouldn't be in my life for long. He'd probably think I was young, weak, and stupid, probably because I had been.

He narrowed his eyes at me. "Actually, it is my business. If you're suffering from some kind of post-traumatic stress disorder, I need to know about it—before the hit. It could affect things."

I glared at him, and he had the nerve to chuckle. "I'm not as stupid as I look. I'm actually not stupid at all, Nixie baby."

"Says the quake addict," I retorted snidely. "Because getting addicted to anything points to all kinds of smarts."

Epic dropped his gaze from mine and frowned. "We all have our demons."

Now that intrigued me. What kind of demons did he have that would push him to use quake?

Maybe Epic isn't the Neanderthal thug that I think he is.

I shook my head to dislodge that thought. There I go again, trying to give people more credit than they deserve. Not everyone has layers of complicated deepness to them. Some people are one dimensional and you get what you see. I'd learned that lesson from Teddy too. I thought Teddy had some kind of profound pain under the surface, some level of emotional deepness that he tried to hide with his attitude problem. And, of course, I had also thought I could be the one who brought it out and healed him. Instead, I found out just how horribly wrong I had been.

"I don't really care about your demons, Epic."

"But I care about yours. I need to know if your condition and will it affect . . . the heist," Epic persisted.

The heist? Sure. He wants to know if it will affect him getting closer to me. What other reason can it be?

"Okay, fine. I have some baggage. But who doesn't. I cope, and I don't use drugs to do it." My voice was starting to get shrill and I hated that he knew he was getting to me.

"Just tell me what happened to you."

"Fine, you want to know what happened to me. I fell in love with the wrong guy. I trusted him. And when I realized he wasn't who I thought he was, I tried to leave, but it was too late. He wouldn't let me." A sob erupted from my chest as the images of him burning me rushed through my mind. I'd spent so much time pushing those memories back into the secret areas of my brain and there they came after a few questions.

"Tell me, Nix." He wiped the tears away from my eyes. "I won't judge you, baby. You've helped me so much. I won't think any worse of you.

I gulped in a load of dread. "Teddy decided that I belonged to him, that I would never be allowed to leave him. He wanted to punish me for even thinking of escaping him. He . . . he . . ." Flashes of Teddy's dark eyes glittering with amusement as he heated the lighter skidded across my mind and I shuddered. "He kept me prisoner, raped, and beat me. And toward the end, he burned me and not just on my arms or legs. He burned me in areas that it took years and lots of enhancement surgery to fix."

I couldn't even have kids. That was how much damage he'd done. Even though the flames didn't go all the way inside me, he'd ruined me to the core. Tears ran down my face and I raised a hand to wipe at them with bewilderment. I hadn't realized I had any tears left to shed over what had happened to me.

"I still have scars in many places. I never could afford all of the enhancements. It took lots of hustling to get my face fixed and then my legs and breasts." I closed my eyes. "Fixing the other places took even longer."

"You said he's dead, right?" Epic growled.

"Yes."

"I wish he was alive. I'd melt his skin, let him heal, and then do it again."

I displayed a pitiful smile. "My own special psycho."

"That's right, Nixie baby."

I spread my legs open and exposed the scars on the edge of my bikini line. I ran my fingertips along the raised ridges on my inner thighs. They stood out a light white color in contrast to my olive-toned skin. The jagged marks rose half an inch.

"Oh God, Nixie. I'm so sorry."

"I survived. That's the whole point. I survived." I turned around and lay on my stomach. "There are scars all over my back. I couldn't afford any more surgeries so I decided to cover it up. Naturally, I couldn't do electric tattooing."

"It burns as the color is applied."

"Yeah. It was too close to that time. I couldn't relive it. But truthfully, I saved the marks on my back for last, even when I had the money to fix them. I wanted them to remain there on my body."

"Why didn't you want to remove them?'

"Because I never wanted to forget—I never wanted to make the mistake of trusting someone like him again." My whole body shook as if I were cold, and I couldn't seem to stop it. "And the marks on my back was the last time he burned me, before I pushed his own flames against his face and set him on fire. You couldn't even imagine the feeling of freedom and the rush of relief as I watched him burn."

The muscle in Epic's jaw twitched. "Where did you hide his body?"

"I didn't. I set his whole apartment on fire and never returned."

"And the phoenix ink is because of him too."

Not a question, I noticed, but a statement. Somehow Epic had gotten me to spill my biggest secret with hardly any effort. *What is it about him that gets to me?* More tears streamed down my face, much to my dismay, and I ran my hands up and down my arms to stop myself from shaking, but sadly, it wasn't doing any good.

Suddenly I was surrounded by Epic's warm body, his delicious, spicy scent swirling around me. I raised my hand to push him away, but he pulled me into him tighter and kissed the top of my head. "It's okay, Nixie baby. It'll be okay."

For some reason, the emotional dam inside me broke and I began to sob in earnest. Pain tremored through my body. Epic pulled me back into bed with him and held me tightly against his chest. His heartbeat thumped in my ears. I continued to sob. He stroked my hair and murmured words, ones that pacified the slivers of fear that cut into my heart, words that caressed something deep inside my soul. That odd self-destructing part of me pondered if I was being stupid, letting him comfort me, but it felt so good to let go and to feel completely safe for once. So I let him reassure me and massage my back with his hands until I eventually fell asleep and dreamed of us, together, far off on a secluded planet, just him and me making love under the moonlit sky.

CHAPTER 11
EPIC

I stood on the hotel balcony, feeling renewed. Nix had rented us a room on the twelfth floor, which gave us a great view of the aerial expressway.

Being off quake made everything seem clearer.

Color exploded everywhere in bright shades. I snapped pictures with my eyes when something captivated me. Lush trees stacked with leaves dipped in a deep cobalt blue. Stark white smeared the glorious sky. Violet birds flew by with crooked lilac beaks. The sun burned gold. The streets cried silver metal and gleamed with polished surfaces.

People zoomed by on small personal hovercrafts. The tiny machines looked like floating scooters as men and women stood on the contraptions with their hands on the handles in front of them. A few wore various types of helmets—huge plastic things that wrapped around their heads with straps. The cooler helmets had designs done in blinking lights. A few aerial cars rushed by in the farther lane as if they weren't allowed to drive on the same path with the personal hovers.

How much does it cost to get your own personal hover?

And the people, Holy Duchess, they were different than anything I'd ever seen. I didn't get to see many other species on earth. The planet didn't receive a lot of tourists once the president agreed to the landfill deal. There were mainly three types of groups who tended to visit earth. The really poor—so broke they had nowhere to live and so they traveled to earth and worked menial jobs for little pay. Busloads of middle-grade students came, escorted by teachers, to hover over the landfills and learn about the consequences of waste and not recycling. Finally, star lords trafficking drugs made weekly drops to all the continents on the planet. But no one else really arrived to vacation or tour.

Especially not people like the ones who'd driven in front of me.

Lime-green skin coated most of the drivers. Brown freckles dusted their foreheads and noses. *Do they speak English? And do they talk out of their mouths?* I hadn't seen any lips, just a line under their pointed nose. I assumed the creatures came in male and female. My old biology teacher had preached that almost all species across the galaxy possessed male and female form, except for one: Crohs. They boasted three genders, female, male, and the last one called nun that merged the sexual organs together. If I remembered correctly, the only way the Crohs could reproduce was a connection of all three united together.

I laughed as I spotted a few Crohs among the traffic. They stood tall compared to any other. Dark black skin stretched over their bony bodies. Silver filled their eyelids.

They possessed no hair. One beeped at me. I had no idea what gender it was, but I raised my hand in greeting anyway.

Women with seductive smiles waved at me as they drove by. Their fingers glittered with jewels. Classy fabrics wavered against their body as the wind stirred their clothes. A few hooted at me with an air of independence. Perfume drifted my way, the expensive kind, the type that signaled the wearer had the cubes to purchase it and more. I winked at a few.

"You might want to put some clothes on, lover boy," Nix's voiced sounded behind me.

And suddenly all those women blurred into nothing. All those expensive perfumes evaporated into Nix's alluring scent of jasmine and roses. A shiver traveled through my body, awakening my flesh. I breathed her in and licked my lips, but couldn't turn around yet.

Early that morning, I'd woken up to my arms around her body. Only a thin piece of material concealed those soft breasts against my chest. She inhaled and exhaled as she slept. Even her breath held a note of something sweet, like she'd been eating ripe peaches the whole night. My dick shifted to hard steel in seconds. It took every bit of strength I had left to unfold myself from her firm body, leave the warm bed, and escape to the balcony. Because the last thing I wanted to do was wake up the woman who'd helped nursed me through withdrawal for three days and shove my dick into her unsuspecting center.

I can't force myself on her or try to take advantage of her.

Not when she'd let her guard down with me and confessed her secret and tortured past. I couldn't be that bastard that walked through her nightmares. She deserved more.

"Good morning, Nixie baby." I slipped my hands into my boxer briefs and adjusted myself to hide my erection. The urge to slide my thumb against the mushroomed tip of my dick hit me hard, but I forced myself to calm down. That was all I needed to do, masturbate on the balcony in front of Nix and planet Trinity's commuters. I'd be locked up by the end of the night. "Did I wake you?"

"Nope. Your amorous fans did," she replied.

"They weren't that loud."

"Really? Every time someone honked, I figured a pair of panties was being added to the pile."

Laughing, I faced her. "No. I haven't had panties thrown at me since I performed on stage."

"You sang?"

"Yes."

The sun shined on her face, highlighting her eye lashes with golden light and causing those emerald eyes to gleam. *Breathtaking.* She wore a tight pink shirt and matching shorts. I didn't figure her for a lady that wore pink, but the color radiated a hard edge on her. She seemed even more dangerous as her nipples pushed against the fabric.

"What's going on in that devious mind of yours?" She quirked her perfectly arched eyebrows.

"Thank you for taking care of me."

"Your battle with quake isn't over. Some say it takes a month to even begin controlling the cravings and a year to start forgetting it."

I let my gaze stray to those plump nipples, before dragging my attention back to her. "Are you telling me you want to stay in this room with me for a month? It could get boring, although I have some suggestions for entertainment."

"Yeah, I bet you do." She tucked midnight strands behind her ear. "It might be time to focus on why you're here."

"I don't know. After all of this honking and your helping me get over quake, perhaps you can show me how to catch a female whale." *Maybe that will stop me from drooling over you.* "Do you think I have what it takes?"

I spread out my arms and twirled around. Someone honked behind me. Nix trailed her gaze from my head to my toes and then frowned.

I shrugged. "I guess that frown is a no."

"Maybe." She captured her bottom lip with her teeth. I craved to suck on that lip as she pierced it with no restraint.

Fuck. I got off quake to now be hooked on Nix.

"Whose picture is in that locket?" She pointed to the heart monitor I wore on a chain that my mother had bought me for my tenth birthday.

"No one's picture is in there." I didn't want to say what it really was. It was dumb enough to get addicted to a crazy drug like quake, even more stupid to do the drug while you had a heart problem. Granted, I hadn't had a heart attack in ten years, but the possibility always remained lurking within the shadows.

Chuckling to myself, I stepped around her, went inside the hotel room, and headed to my jeans. "How much did this room cost you?"

From the open balcony doorway, she watched me pull out my wallet. "Don't worry about it. Just start focusing on business and mainly our hit."

"That's my plan." I yanked out several hundred cubes. The silver disks smoothed against my hand. I set them on the table. "Meanwhile, take this to relieve some of the guilt I have for you taking care of me."

"It was nothing. Really."

I looked into her eyes. "It meant a whole lot to me. I stood outside of that cab like an idiot, ready to run in the other direction and buy some quake. And there you came, saving the day and bossing my big bozo brothers around."

"Like I said. It was nothing." She twisted the end of her shirt with her fingers. I wondered if it was a nervous habit. Up until this moment I didn't think she got nervous.

I stepped toward her. "I owe you."

"Yes, you do. But I'm not accepting anything less than the amount of a quarter million cubes." She backed up and narrowed her eyes at me. "That payoff is the real reason why I babysat you while you detoxed, nothing else. We're just business partners."

"I know."

"Do you now?" She gestured to my erection. "And what about him? Does he know that my tender side was bought on by the quarter million cubes in my future, and nothing more?"

I flashed a wicked grin. "Him and I both understand. But give him a break. I'm only human, after all. You're fucking hot and your scent is intoxicating. Plus it's been a while since I had sex."

"Well, don't expect me to offer. I thanked you with that friendly little mouth hug. You should count yourself lucky, because that's all you'll be getting from me in this lifetime, lover boy." She crossed her arms around her chest and scowled at me. My dick pressed against my boxers' fabric.

Why did she have to remind me of that mouth hug? As if it could be called something so trivial.

I stalked by her. "I'm going to take care of my horniness tonight. Until then, I'm taking a shower."

"Why not just take care of your horniness now—in the shower?" she asked behind me.

Leave it to Nixie to suggest I yank my cock off without feeling embarrassed or weird about the topic.

"Thanks, but I'm particular about the act. I prefer a warm and wet body under me." I entered the mint-colored bathroom with a television screen mounted inside the wall of the shower. I pressed the button near the light switch. The TV flashed on to the news. I pushed the mute button since there was a trail of words at the bottom of the screen that informed the viewer what was being said. I kept the channel there, figuring the news would be a great way to familiarize myself with the planet.

"So you're going to find some chick to nail and bail tonight?" Nix positioned herself next to the sink as I opened the shower's glass door."

"I'll have Shade watch the kids tonight, hit a club, grab a girl, do her somewhere, and then return home."

"Just like that, huh?" She rolled her eyes.

"Did you miss the news that I was the hottest stud in this galaxy?" I pulled off my boxer briefs. She gazed at my ass and made no attempt to hide it. I'd expected nothing less from such a bold and confident woman. A beep sounded when I stepped in, signaling the shower had sensed my presence and would now be computing my height, weight, body frame, and anything else the machine thought it required in order to better assist me with my cleansing process. The walls hummed. The shower floor glowed green.

"Good morning, sir. What temperature of water would you prefer?" A male voice came from the ceiling.

K.D. PENN

"Warm." I turned and was surprised to see Nix still there. My erection pointed her way as if pleading with her to come over. She focused on it and licked her lips. Scorching-hot lust sprang from the tip of my dick, glided down the shaft, encased my balls, and spread up across the rest of my body.

She needs to leave before I take her in this bathroom.

A tiny line of water spilled out of the ceiling and tapped against my chest.

"Is this temperature to your liking sir?" the male voice asked.

"Make it a few degrees hotter."

Nix's eyes went to mine as she cleared her throat.

Hot water sprayed out of the ceiling and poured over me. The soothing liquid streamed down my face, traveling over my biceps and rows of muscles around my waist. When the heat of the shower arrived at my dick, I groaned, but kept my hands to my side.

Nix stepped to the shower door and pressed her hands against the glass surface. "You should just . . . take care of yourself now."

"And why should I?" I switched my eyes' zoom valve on and pushed the view toward her stiff nipples as they rubbed against the glass.

"Going to a club where there will most definitely be drugs is going to be too much for you too soon." She centered her attention on my cock, the tip of it to be exact. The whole time, she slid her tongue inch by inch along the top of her lip. "Grab that bottle of shampoo over there."

I returned my eyes to normal view. "And if I don't?"

"I don't know. Maybe I'll shoot you again." She edged away from the glass door and yanked off her shirt. Two full and heavy breasts appeared with pink nipples that puckered out like someone had been sucking on them all day. The shirt dropped to the floor. I rushed to the glass door. She put out her hand to stop me and wagged her finger. "Not so fast, lover boy. Don't get presumptuous on me. I already told you that my mouth hug was all you'd ever get from me."

"Take off those shorts," I growled. "Maybe I should give that plump bud between your thighs a mouth hug."

Her lips quivered. She backed up into the wall. "I'm not interested in having your mouth between my legs. Besides, you can't give a female a mouth hug."

"Says who?"

"Says me. I created the term."

"Just one lick, please," I begged and almost lowered down to my knees. "I've wanted to taste you since I met you. Ever since you rocked those hips back and forth on that stage."

"No."

"You hypnotized me, Nixie. You've been on my mind ever since. Not even quake could keep you out of it."

"You're full of shit. You really think I'm going to buy that line of crap from you?" she whispered.

"No wonder it was you that helped me get off quake. All I needed was you near me and the craving for it left. Let me taste you."

"Not going to happen." She sighed and then targeted me with her gaze. "Now get that shampoo or I leave this bathroom and you'll never know what I was planning for you. I'm thinking you might like it."

I cursed under my breath, searched the shelf on the right, and grabbed the shampoo. Other bottles fell to the floor and splashed water around me.

"Now, pour the shampoo all over that big, delicious cock of yours." She pressed the button for the television and turned it off.

As if I could be distracted by a damn television when her huge tits are naked and in front of me.

I leaned back on the wall and poured the shampoo on me. Hot water continued to rain down on my skin. "Shower, turn off."

The shower ceased, leaving beads of water all over my flesh. I lathered my dick with the cool amber liquid, loving the silky texture. My balls clenched. Nix watched with parted lips. The fragrance of peaches rose around me and reminded me of Nix's breathing earlier that morning when I held her in bed.

"Next I want you to start stroking that glorious erection while you look at me." Nix placed her hands on her waist and glided her fingers slowly up to her breasts and then over those pink erect points.

"You're so fucking hot." I wrapped my hand around my dick and moved my fingers little by little along the shaft, savoring the rough feel of my skin and relishing in the beauty before me. The temperature of my body lifted higher than a hot shower could ever increase it. I shuddered and was starving for her satin flesh or just a sample of what flavor lay between her damp folds. She had to be wet and warm. I craved to see her pussy, inhale its scent, lick it, and would have sold all my worth just to rub my mouth along her clit.

"Pay attention."

"Trust me. I am paying attention, more than you know."

She lifted one of her breasts until the nipple rose to her mouth. "Tell me what you want, Epic."

"I want you to lick that plump nipple. I need to see that magical tongue." I squeezed the head of my cock and groaned. Her wet pink tongue lapped at that nipple like it had been dipped in sugar. Pre-cum spurted from my dick and mixed in with the foam of the shampoo. She pinched the other nipple with her free hand while wiggling the tip of her tongue along that blushing rose-colored areola.

"Damn the Duchess!" I dropped my dick and pushed the glass door open.

"No." She let go of her breasts and wagged her finger at me. "You don't get to touch me."

"Please." My insides charged with a searing yearning. I almost cried. I wanted her so much, needed her under me. "Do you want me to beg?"

She responded with a wicked giggle. "Actually, I wouldn't mind seeing you beg. In fact, I think I might really enjoy seeing a big muscular alpha male such as yourself—on your knees, hard as a rock, and begging to let you fuck me. That would be extremely hot. "

"I'd do it." I formed my fingers into fists. "I'd do what-ever you want just to push my tongue inside of you."

She stirred, but her face shifted to a blank expression. "Don't bother. It'd be a waste of your time. Time to close the shower door so you get back to a little bit of self-loving."

Pouting, I slammed the door back. She would be the death of me. This woman with a tiny, seductive frame who appeared so fragile and in need was a beast of a lady. She could devour me, spit my crumbled soul out, and then sashay those seductive hips to her next victim.

And, still, I'll stay here.

I returned to caressing myself in my hand.

What else can I do? Clearly she's the boss when my dick's concerned.

"Focus, Epic."

I groaned. "What do you want me to do now, you little teasing trek?"

She winked. "There's no need to be so mean. At least I'm going to let you see what you're missing. It's more than most men get. I may be a tease, but I'm teasing you better than the rest, baby."

A grumble emitted from my throat.

"Fine." She displayed a mocking pout and placed her hands on the waist band of her shorts. "You have been an obedient patient for me. And you take directions quite well. You ready for your gift?"

My mouth watered as if the greatest feast was set before me. "Yes. I'll take whatever you're willing to give."

"So you're saying you want to see my pussy?" she whispered and leaned back on the wall. "You want me to pull these shorts down and open my legs for you to see me completely laid bare before you?"

"Yes, Nixie baby. Show me that sweet pussy." I rubbed my hand up and down my dick, tightening my grip and letting the pressure hit the rim of my head. My senses shivered in anticipation. I could feel my orgasm materialize in my core and begin to ascend.

"You said you loved it when I danced on stage? Do you want me to dance for you now?" Slowly, she wound her hips from side to side like a spellbinding snake. Her breasts jiggled with the movement. "Ask nicely. Say please."

"Please," I cried. "Please, dammit. Please."

"Put all of your fingers around your dick and fuck them hard. Pretend that you're thrusting deep inside of me—pretend you're fucking me and not your hands." She rocked her body and slipped down the shorts no more than an inch.

I followed her orders with anticipation. All of my fingers tightened around my erection like tight fists. I thrust fast into my hands, with power and lust-filled violence, imagining I was inside her. It felt so good, like I could explode in seconds. A moan ripped from my lips.

"Say my name." Desire gleamed in her eyes. She knew what she was doing to me and loved it. *She has to.* Here I was, three times her size, and hovering over her with my hands on my dick, just waiting for her next order.

"Go faster." She smirked. "I want to see you fall to pieces right in front of me, I want to see you ripped apart by your need while I watch you."

"You'll be seeing a lot more than that," I hissed as my dick moved through my big hands. "I'm going to paint this glass with my cum."

"Hmmm. Really? Wouldn't you rather paint my face with it? Watch it slide down my chin . . . maybe witness me taste it with my tongue. Would you like that?"

God, yes.

"Nixie," I moaned and my pace sped up. I tightened my buttocks as I plunged my dick deeper between my hands. The muscles on my thighs burned. "Oh God, Nixie, please let me see it. Damn you. I need to see it."

She pulled the shorts down. Her olive folds came into my view. Lush and thick. No hair, just smooth skin. Moistness glistened around the split opening. And I was sure she was wet and ready for me. She lifted her leg up and balanced it on the sink next to her. Her plump pink clit peeked out as those taunting lips widened.

"Fuck!" I came hard. Warm semen burst from my dick and sprayed the glass. I thrust harder. "Damn you, you're too fucking hot."

More spilled, yet I remained hard and still hungry. I released my dick, pushed open the glass, fell on my knees, and buried my mouth between her thighs. She didn't even stop me. *How could she?* She was dripping with need. I lapped at her, dipping my tongue in her tunnel, and then gliding it to her bud. I sucked on her clit, loving the way she tasted and the velvet texture of her flesh.

"Epic," she moaned, rubbing and rocking into my face. Her natural fragrance captured me. She grabbed my long, wet hair in her hands and held on to me.

"That's right, baby. Put this sweet pussy all over me." I stabbed her with my tongue, plunging it deep into her. She screamed and ground into me hard. Her body trembled under me. She fell back. I grabbed her ass with my hands and kept her up and balanced. It was like she didn't care or notice that she'd almost fallen as she fucked my tongue with no restraint and self-control. And I was glad. I owed her more than I could give, more than I was worth.

"Don't stop!" she shrieked.

Never.

I moved my tongue in and out of her until she clasped her walls around it and screamed. Her arousal spread through and spasmed into her. *So sweet.* I had to hold her completely as her legs went limp.

"Fuck." She tried to climb out of my hands, but I kept my grip on her behind. Before I rose, I planted kisses on the scars on her bikini line. I loved all of Nix, from that smart, bossy mouth down to the marks of her dark past, and anything in between. I planted my mouth on her wounds and she shuddered.

"Stop," she whimpered.

Licking my lips, I stood. She climbed away from me with shivering fingers.

"I love hearing you scream my name." I leaned in to kiss her.

She moved her lips out of my reach. "Motherfucker. You weren't supposed to do that."

"Do what? Tell me what I did." I pulled her into me. My stiff cock pressed against her stomach. She trembled under me while my body smoothed against hers. "I could lick you all day. When I'm a rich man, I'd love for you to consider letting me spend my days and nights between your thighs."

"No. I'm not interested." She didn't look into my eyes. Instead, she focused on the area behind me. "Let me go—now."

I released her. "Did I do something wrong? I thought you liked it."

Ignoring my question, she bent over, grabbed her shorts, and yanked them up. "We check out in an hour. I'll meet you at your house tonight."

I edged back. "What will you be doing in between us checking out and when you meet me at the house?"

"Pappy is showing me around the planet today. I've put him off as long as I can if I don't want him to move on to someone more eager. You don't need me to babysit you constantly, now that the worst is over." She glared at me as if challenging me to say something.

It was like a wall shot up between us. One minute I was licking between her thighs. The next instance, she was talking to me like I was some stranger she'd just met.

Although rage coursed through my veins, I battled with myself to not yell or argue.

What the hell did I think was going to happen?

Some monster of a guy had imprisoned and tortured her. Her whole head had to be messed up. I should be happy she didn't attack me when I rushed out of the shower. *I'll never have her the way I crave her.* And it was best I got that in my head as soon as possible.

"So I'll be with Pappy the rest of the day."

"Then I'll meet with you tonight." I placed my hands behind my back and clamped them into tight fists. She raised her eyebrows, but didn't say anything.

You want a fight, don't you? A reason to stomp away from me filled with rage. I won't give it to you. Deal with it.

"I'm glad you'll give me your time tonight. I'll have my cousin come to the house. You should meet him. He's a manager for Dynamics, the club we're going to rob. He's the one bringing me on as a bouncer and you as a dancer." I wished she would put her shirt back on. It was getting too difficult to not stare at those nipples and lick my lips. "Is eight tonight good for you?"

She opened her mouth and closed it as if she'd been ready to say something else and was caught off guard. "Umm . . . yes. Pappy and I should be done by then."

Pappy and you?

Visions of snapping Pappy's neck filled my head. "Good. I hope you can make it."

She covered her breasts and turned to leave.

"Nix."

She paused with her back to me. I didn't mind. Her position gave me a great view of her curvy behind, the one I'd just had in my hands moments before. Her tattoo gleamed in the light. With this close of a view, I could now see the scars painted with black and orange. They formed the fire around the phoenix as it escaped.

"What do you want, Epic?"

"If this Pappy or any other man harms you, then call or come to me," I said through clenched teeth.

"I'm a fully grown woman who is perfectly capable of taking care of herself. In fact, I prefer to be on my own."

"It doesn't matter. You helped me when I needed it. I'll help you if you need me to." I stepped closer to her and saw her shoulders tense, so I made sure not to touch her. "Remember this. No matter what happens from now until after this hit, you'll always have me, a deranged psycho, willing to tear off the dick of any guy that bothers you and smash the remains into his chest cavity."

"My own personal psycho at my beck and call?"

"Always, Nixie baby. Anytime. Any day." I swallowed down my fear and pulled up my courage as I said the next words, "And if you need me for more—love when you're lost and alone, sex when you're horny, tender kisses just to realize another cares, I'll be there for you without asking any questions or assuming that you're mine."

"I can . . . take care of myself." Her voice cracked at the end.

I wished I could see the look on her face and wondered what thoughts ran through her head. "I'm not the guy from your past. Only a monster would cage an exotic bird that was birthed for freedom and flying."

She sighed.

"I don't want to suffocate you. I just sometimes want to be in the air that you breathe and know that in those few seconds I'm the one on your mind."

She hurried away without a reply—or more like fled. I remained where I was and made myself get back in the shower. *I bet she'll be gone by the time I'm done in here.* The feeling that I pushed too far hit me square in the gut, like someone punched the darkness out of me. Yet I had no regrets for what I'd said. She needed to know I yearned to have her in my life some way. I wasn't wishing for a girlfriend or wife, but I damn sure craved something more.

But what do I want? I don't know.

The concept was more a sensation in my chest verses a clear defined word or thought. Standing in the shower, I smelled her scent on my hands and tasted her cum on my lips. My dick twitched. My body awakened with new stimulation as if I hadn't come in years.

If she was a drug, I'd lock myself in a dark room and snort her all day.

But she wasn't. She was a woman that had survived more pain than any grown man could bear. She'd done it and moved on without taking up a drug habit like me or sinking down into defeat like most. I yearned to have her all to myself, to keep her next to me all day and night.

But in the end, she was a bird that craved flight, expanding her wings out into the open sky, until the cool wind carried her higher into the clouds, far from harm. As much as my dick, heart, and mind screamed cage her, I couldn't.

CHAPTER 12
PHOENIX

"So what do you think, my dear?" Pappy's bland voice pierced my thoughts.

"What?"

"What do you think of Trinity?" Pappy spread out his arms to encompass the view before him. "I'm sure this is a bit prettier than earth. I've heard there is even garbage in the ocean."

"Not yet, but close." I combed my fingers through my hair and forced my eyes to take in the scenery before me.

It was a magnificent view. We stood on an observation deck mounted with platinum bricks. Twin full moons glittered in the soft radiance of the magenta sky. Sky crafts zoomed through the air but we were so high up my view of the alien sky was completely unfettered. It was stunning, beautiful, and enchanting, yet I couldn't seem to truly see anything except Epic's chiseled face.

A huge beach rested before us. Waves crashed against the rocky cliffs. I couldn't make out most of the color, but the water brightened from the things that swam inside it. Kind of like the fish had little lights attached to their scales, and when they glowed, the whole sea lit up in the night.

Silk curtains draped the glass doors behind us to give us some privacy from the restaurant diners who sat inside. A savory aroma drifted out to me, but I wasn't hungry. My gut twisted and turned into itself with all that had happened the last days.

Epic's words floated in my head. *And if you need me for more—love when you're lost and alone, sex when you're horny, tender kisses just to realize another cares, I'll be there for you without asking any questions or assuming that you're mine.*

I sighed. *Damn you, Epic.*

A waiter stepped out from between the curtains. I doubted he was even human. His skin glowed lime green. Brown dots scattered across most of his face. He had no lips, just slits that spread from ear to ear. Instead of the usual black-and-white one-piece suit most servants wore in restaurants on earth, he wore gold plastic jacket with no shirt or matching pants. "Mabr tun v-vdrak bonon?"

"Yes. I would love a small glass of your finest scotch. Three cubes of ice." Pappy turned to me. "Darling, what would you like to drink?"

I don't want to suffocate you. I just sometimes want to be in the air that you breathe and know that in those few seconds I'm the one on your mind.

"Darling?" Pappy tapped my shoulder. "Are you sure you're okay?"

"Yes. I'm so sorry. What did you ask me?"

"What would you like to drink?"

"Something strong."

Pappy faced the waiter. "Give her a nice scotch too with some ice—"

"No ice, please. Just a splash of mineral water. Not the sparkling kind." I waved my hand.

The waiter nodded. "Mabr gor. Mabr tek v-vaynoc."

"Correct," Pappy said as the waiter left.

"What language is that?" I asked, hoping to make up for my odd behavior. I'd been ignoring him all day and was sure he was getting suspicious. Soon my whale would swim off to another fisher-woman with less boggled-down thoughts and a more attentive attitude.

"He's a Vox, native to this planet. He spoke in his language. Yet, as you can see, he understands English and most languages quite well." Pappy twisted the ends of his curly mustache and then released it. "The problem is that Vox mouths make it almost impossible to sound out most of the phonetics in English, so he speaks in his language."

"Interesting."

"I've been living on Trinity for almost twenty years. I learned their language after two years." Pappy beamed. "I've picked up a few things."

"That's one of the reasons why I'm here, to pick at that valuable mind of yours. I hope to gain a lot from you and maybe give in return." I trailed my index finger from his forehead to his cheek. He quivered under my touch. *I think that got his attention.* He cleared his throat and held out his arm. I hooked my own arm around his and he guided me to the edge of the observation deck.

"Let's get a closer look," he said.

A few feet closer and I realized that instead of just air and nothing in front of us, there was a solid glass wall all around the balcony, probably so no one would fall. I rested my free arm on it and drank in the sight. How captivating it was, like a scene from a romantic movie right as the hero and heroine come together and kiss. I'd dreamed of moments like that happening for me around a precious landscape similar to the one before us, but not with a man like Pappy. Sure, he was a nice guy and soaked in money, but he didn't resemble the heroes of my dreams, the ones who captured my heart and imprisoned my soul with theirs.

But then Teddy came along.

And most of my dreams shifted into nightmares filled with flames and smoke. I stopped fantasizing about heroes and transformed those foolish love wishes into possible plots for money. So here I stood next to a rich man who was willing to do anything for me and provide me almost instantly with the things I desired. *I should be happy.* Gloom unfurled inside my chest and pounded with the beat of my heart.

Only a monster would cage an exotic bird that was birthed for freedom and flying.

I should never have let him touch me. *That was a huge mistake.* He was getting under my skin in a most annoying way. *Damn him. I won't let him ruin this for me.*

"This sky is why people all over the galaxy travel so far to see it." Pappy broke the silence between us. "What do you think, darling?"

I forced the best smile I could manage and turned to face Pappy. "It's absolutely amazing. Thank you so much for bringing me here."

The waiter returned and handed us our drinks with his glowing green hands. "Bron tor v-vadrak."

"Yes. We'll let you know if we need anything else." Pappy took a tiny sip of his scotch as it chilled in a violet glass shaped like a tube.

I put my own tube to my lips. The cold glass froze my lips a bit. I tipped my head back and swallowed all the scotch in one gulp. The frosty liquid burned as it traveled down my throat. My chest warmed. I coughed a little and snapped my fingers at the waiter before he left. "I'd like another one of those, please."

The waiter bowed and vanished within the curtains.

Pappy eyed me speculatively. "What's wrong, my darling Nix? You've seemed distant all day." He reached up and tucked my hair behind my ear on the left side of my head. I had to suppress the urge to back away from his touch. "Are you worried about your brother?"

I choked back a snort. If he only knew the kinds of thoughts I'd been thinking about my supposed brother all day, Pappy would probably have a heart attack. I bit the inside of my cheek and sighed wistfully. "I must confess that I am stressed about his drug use."

"Of course you are."

"I guess. It's just hard to enjoy all of this fully when I know my brother is still getting over his addiction."

My mind conjured up an image of Epic's dark lustful gaze staring up the line of my body as he licked my heated center. My knuckles tightened on the observation deck railing. Maybe I had a new addiction of my own. *Epic.* I cringed. Of course he wasn't the first man since Teddy who'd piqued my hormone's interest. But he was the first that seemed to be needling his way into my heart somehow. His words had haunted me all day and this evening. Images of his mouth doing its magic below me had corroded my brain waves.

I can't let this continue. I have to get him off my mind. I can't let a man like Epic get into my system any further.

"I understand, darling. I had a distant cousin that battled a drug addiction for many years." Pappy ran his clammy hand down my arm and again, I resisted the urge to pull away from him. "I let him stay at one of my condos on the other side of Trinity and he ended up stealing everything out of it to buy his mess. And later he had a poor family of Vox renting my condo out and giving him the money. It was a disaster and misfortunate for the whole family."

"I can't even imagine." I feigned interest.

"Well, Mother refused to speak to him again and forbid his side of the family from vacationing with us on holidays."

"That seems a bit drastic."

"Well, you can't coddle addicts, darling. Trust me. I know a lot of things."

I doubt you know as much as me.

I frowned, realized I was doing it, and formed my lips into a smile.

"Oh dear. I'm so selfish." He patted my head like I was a puppy. "Do you want to call it a night then? We can have another date tomorrow maybe?"

I shook my head vehemently. "No, no—let me just go freshen up. I'm not going to let Epic ruin our day."

I ground my teeth together as I said Epic's name because again his gorgeous face flashed in front of my mind's eye. *Damn him.* I didn't like the idea of hanging out with Pappy for another minute, but if the date ended, I'd have to face Epic sooner. I didn't think I was ready for that yet. I just needed more time to think, or rather, *not think* about him.

"I really am enjoying our time together." I grabbed his hand. "I'm learning so much."

"Are you sure?"

"Yes. Just let me go and freshen up some more in the ladies' room. Is that what they call it here on Trinity?"

He chuckled. "Well, it's called *shor tun* in Vox."

"Shor tun?"

"Good job." Pappy squeezed my hand as he gave me a patronizing smile. "Alright. I'll be right here waiting for you."

"Thanks." I smiled briefly before scampering off in the other direction to find the ladies' room.

After pushing through the silk curtains, I stepped into the dining area of the restaurant. White light bathed the space and reflected off the shiny silver walls. The allure of savory food teased my senses. People filled the tables all over the room. Leather corsets of many colors draped the women. Soft, lush fabrics flowed out from their corsets and hid their legs. Most of the men had mustaches just like Pappy. Some fluffed out in a bushy sweep. Others thinned over the lips, but all of them curled up at the ends. More green waiters journeyed throughout the dining area, carrying trays of food and drinks in their hands.

I departed from the dining room and entered a dimly lit hallway. No one walked it but me. I hoped a bathroom was at the end or at least a path to a bathroom.

"I'll be there for you without asking any questions or assuming that you're mine."

Yeah, yeah, he says that now, but how long would that be enough, before he demanded more from me? Guys like him always want more than I want or can give.

I was so lost in my thoughts of Epic that I nearly ran face first into—

"Epic!" I exclaimed as I looked up from his massive chest that I had almost knocked myself out on. Black leather draped his muscular body. His jacket fit around his chest and arms. His pants formed around his toned thighs. For one brief moment joy burst within my chest, but then the realization that he stood in front of me while Pappy sat out on the observation deck waiting for me yanked me out of my happy moment.

"What in the darkness are you doing here?" I demanded as my smile morphed into a scowl.

He had the nerve to toss me a wicked smile, one that dripped with sex and sensual promises. *And since when does he have dimples?*

"I'm watching your back—making sure nothing happens to you." He reached up and tucked some of my hair behind my ear, much like Pappy just had, but instead of being slightly skeeved out, my body hummed with anticipation.

"I'm not a fan of stalkers. If you think doing this is going to endear you to me—"

Epic slid one hand down my back to rest just above my ass and took a few steps backward so we were hidden in the shadows of an alcove just off from my destination of the ladies' room. "Have you been enjoying yourself today?"

I met his lustful eyes as I responded, "My day has been absolutely amazing." I hated how sultry my voice sounded. Maybe he wouldn't notice.

"It didn't look that way to me."

"Have you been watching me the whole time?"

"Yes. I happened to see you two at the park across from the hotel. He was picking you up in his ugly car, so I decided to grab a cab and follow you two."

"For safety reasons?" I quirked my eyebrows at him.

"Of course. It was all professional motivation, nothing more or less." Epic's statement didn't seem to mirror where his mind really was. The hand that was on my lower back slid down to cup my ass and he pulled me flush against his body. Lust shined over his eyes. He sniffed at the area near my neck and moaned. "Why do you always smell so damn good?"

"Epic, you need to leave. I don't want you here."

"Mmm hmm," Epic murmured as he dropped his head to skim his full lips down the side of my exposed neck. I clutched at his shoulders, willing myself to push him away, but my body had a mind of its own. Epics other hand skimmed the top of my corset, causing my nipples to pebble almost painfully. "Think about how different it would have been if you would have let me show you the planet today instead of Pappy. I trailed you both everywhere. The whole time that boring guy talked and fondled his mustache while you stared off into the sky . . . what were you thinking about?"

"Not you."

"You're lying."

"No. I'm not. I thought you were going to give me space," I practically pleaded. Because if he kept going the way he was now, I'd be putty in his hands in no time. And that was completely unacceptable. "Isn't that what you said back at the hotel?"

"I changed my mind." Epic bit at one of my nipples through the corset. Somehow his teeth managed the form the leather around my point enough to encase it. I moaned with pleasure. He bit down on the leather again and then released it. "I want you, Nixie baby, and I can't stand the thought of Pappy's or anyone's hands on you but mine."

"It's not your choice."

Epic lifted my leg and placed it on his hip. I gasped when his leather-clad dick ground against my hungry core. He slid his hand up my thigh.

"Fuck. You don't have any panties on," Epic growled in my ear.

"I'm well aware," I responded breathily. "Someone could come out and see us. Where's the bathroom?"

"Why? So you can escape?" My back was suddenly pushed against the wall and I heard a zipper being undone. Before I truly had time to process what was going on, Epic's rock-hard cock entered me, slipping up and down through my slick folds briefly first. My whole body shivered with need. But I refused to be a slave to such base desires. I shoved at Epic in protest. His cock slid out of me as he stumbled backward. The head glistened in the dim light. Part of me wanted to slap at it for thinking he could just put it inside me without asking. The other half craved to drop on my knees and suck my wetness off.

He took a step my way.

I held out my hand. "No. I told you this wasn't going to happen again. You think because we swapped some body fluids . . . again, that you own me? I'm telling you once more that I don't belong to anyone. You don't have the right to—"

"You own me," Epic's deep voice rumbled and stopped me short in my tirade.

"What?" I whispered.

Lifting me back up, he returned to stand right in front of me and raised my dress again. If someone came into this hallway, they would see everything and know we were two lovers about to fuck. His dick still pointed toward me under my dress. The throbbing tip teased my clit. Desire twirled at the center of my thighs. I moaned despite myself.

"You own me," he purred. "I'm not taking from you. I'm giving myself to you."

He spread my legs open a little bit wider and entered me again. The pressure of him was just right. A blazing passionate euphoria jolted through every cell of my body.

"You own me." Epic continued to slide his luscious cock between my folds. My heart constricted as his words finally penetrated my consciousness. "You still want me to stop?"

For some reason—I don't know—he'd said exactly the right thing. "Fuck me then. Fuck me now, Epic. If I own you—then I'm telling you to fuck me."

Not having to be told twice, Epic sheathed himself completely inside me in one stroke. We moaned as one. "You feel better than I thought you would—like fucking heaven." Epic groaned so loud I was sure people heard us in the dining area. If Pappy strolled in, my fishing expedition would definitely be over.

"You own every part of me." He thrust hard into me, hitting my cervix just the right way to cause me wet pleasure instead of pain. "Every hair on my head. Every damn inch of skin. My heartbeats. My will. My hunger. My love. You own it all."

"Epic." I gripped his back and urged him on. He built up to a blistering pace that sent me spiraling over the edge of one orgasm after the next in mere minutes. Soon he pumped his own hot release inside me as a long, deep groan erupted from him.

When he was done, he didn't withdraw and instead, buried his face in my hair.

"Nix," he muttered, "I can't believe you just let me fuck you out here."

"Let you?" I laughed.

"I could never overpower you. I felt the gun on the side of your hip right here." He patted it with his hand. "You're a quick draw too. If you didn't want me inside of you, then you would have shot me up with enough siphons to make me detonate with glass."

"Maybe." I gave him a wicked smile.

"Definitely."

"Even though I have the gun, I can't believe I just *let you* fuck me out here either."

"Let's go back to the house, shower, and eat." He pressed his lips against mine, but I didn't return the kiss. I could already feel Epic's hot seed dripping down my inner thighs. It was all too much, too quickly. He wanted more from me than I could give him. Even if I wanted to—and I most certainly didn't. Did he want us to race out of the restaurant like two happy little lovers? And to start dating or something? To become a couple? No. He had a family to take care of and I had myself to worry about.

"I'm not going anywhere. I'll meet you later." I pushed at him and he edged back from me, forcing his cock out of my body. I pulled my skirt down and straightened my clothes. "I better get back to Pappy. He's probably wondering where I am by now."

"Come again," he said through clenched teeth.

"You heard me."

Epic grabbed my arm and I looked up into his scowling features. "No."

"No?" I ground my teeth together. "No what?"

Epic's grip on my arm tightened. "No—you're not going anywhere with Pappy."

"I knew this was a mistake. You didn't mean anything you just said about not owning me, did you? Or did everything change once I let you come inside of me?" I whirled around and stalked back toward the observation deck. "Leave me alone, Epic. What just happened—it never happened as far as I'm concerned."

"You're fucking insane!" he called back as I escaped into the dining area and slammed the door behind me.

Every minute I spend alone with Epic makes me lose brain cells. I refused to let myself get stupid over a man ever again, even if he did seem to know the right things to say. Glancing over my shoulder, I shoved the curtains aside and rushed off onto the observation deck.

"There you are." Pappy's moustache-clad upper lip turned up as I approached him. "I was beginning to worry. You've been gone for a while. Did you find the *shor tun* okay?"

"Yes. I found it with no problem at all." I forced a smile on my face even though I was sure it didn't reach my eyes. I reeked of Epic.

Does Pappy smell it? Can he tell?

"I was just worried. It took some time." Pappy twisted the end of his mustache.

"Sorry, you know there's always a line in the ladies' room."

"Right you are. I don't know what you women do in there, but it takes you all forever to get out of there." Pappy offered me his arm and I slid my hand around to rest on it. "I was thinking you might be hungry. Would you like a nice dinner before we continue our explorations?"

"Yes, I'm actually starving, but I spotted the food in here and wasn't too excited about it. Can we go somewhere else?"

"Of course, darling." I let Pappy lead me to the elevator that would take us to the valet. I glanced around nervously, half expecting Epic to show himself in some kind of testosterone-driven frenzy to claim me. So far there was no sign of him.

But just before the elevator was about to close, Epic slid in and to the side. The elevator was packed and I guessed Pappy hadn't noticed him. *Thank God.* I tried to remain calm, but every muscle in my body tensed. I watched in absolute horror as Epic slid around to stand beside me but slightly diagonal from Pappy. He reached out and took my hand with his but kept his eyes straight ahead. I tried to pull away from him, but there was no good way to make him relinquish my hand without drawing attention to us.

"Darling," Pappy said and I turned my attention to him, "I was thinking after dinner maybe I could show you my house. We could take a dip in the pool or whatever you may wish."

"We'll need to buy me a bathing suit. I didn't bring one with me in our move here."

"That won't be a difficulty at all. Let's buy the swimsuit before we head to dinner."

"That sounds like a lovely idea." I smiled at Pappy even though Epic's grip on my hand had become painfully tight.

"I'd like to pick out the swimsuit."

"Sure, baby, whatever you want." Fuck, was Pappy angling to get me alone and back at his place thinking that he could get laid? I'd excuse myself after dinner for sure, but I certainly wasn't going to let Epic know that.

Pappy grinned at me, lust evident in his eyes. "Gre v-vrat. That means thank you in Vox."

"Interesting."

"I hope to teach you more things." He dabbed at his sweaty moustache with his tongue and I cringed.

The elevator dinged open and people began to spill out. I let Pappy move ahead of me and whirled around to glare at Epic.

"Leave me alone." I hissed under my breath.

"Come back with me." Epic looked so vulnerable that I actually considered it for a millisecond. His eyes shifted from blue to black in seconds.

"No, I'm sorry." Tears pricked at the corners of my eyes. "You don't want me, Epic. I'm broken beyond repair. Just business—we need to keep it just business."

Epic's face fell and he let my hand go. I turned and trailed after Pappy without looking back at Epic. I didn't think I could take it. Tears spilled from my eyes and ran down my face. If I wanted Epic to leave me alone so much, why did the thought of him actually doing it break my heart?

Damn him.

I wanted everything he claimed he could give me. It was just that I knew I could never really have it. I hadn't lied. I was broken. Broken beyond repair, and even if Epic thought he wanted me now, he'd never be able to deal with all my baggage long term. In the end I would end up getting hurt either way. It was best to just leave things the way they were before things got worse.

I caught up to Pappy and intertwined my fingers with his. I had to stifle a shudder because it just felt so different—so wrong after having just had my palm pressed against Epic's.

"I was thinking maybe we should get Italian. Do they have authentic Italian food on Trinity?" I suggested with fake cheer.

"I know just the place, my dear," Pappy said as he led me to his sky craft.

It took only a few minutes for the valet to have the car in front of the restaurant. Epic was nowhere to be found. I slid into the fine leather passenger seat and stared blankly out at the beautiful night sky, which was completely eclipsed by Epic's face and the moment we'd shared in the hallway.

Damn him. I need to stop thinking about him. He's ruining everything.

CHAPTER 13

EPIC

The house I'd rented for my family looked big online, but massive in person. Silver bricks served as the foundation. It towered over the other houses in the neighborhood, so high I figured it may have been three levels instead of the two levels that were advertised. A sleek glass made up the door. I stepped in just as everyone was sitting at the table for dinner.

The triplets raced my way and hugged me. "We missed you so much!"

"I missed you too." I kissed each of their foreheads and grinned.

A rainbow-colored teardrop chandelier hung from the ceiling. All the walls were glass. Some were fogged in shades of red or blue. The walls closer to the back appeared transparent. Scarce furniture scattered around the living room off to the right of the dining room. I headed closer to the silver table.

The kids scrapped purple chunks of meat off their places and shoveled it into their mouths. A honeyed perfume scent drenched the air. I scrunched my face up in horror.

My stomach knotted into disgust. "What's for dinner?"

"It's called fin fin." Mimi's smile widened and brightened more than I'd ever seen before. I hadn't seen her this happy in years.

"Fin fin?"

"It's a popular dish on Trinity. The kids love it 'cause it's so sweet, but it's supposed to be really healthy." She gestured to the bowl of purple gunk in front of her. "You want to try it?"

I patted my stomach. "I'm full. I ate a whole lot where I came from, but maybe I'll try some a little later."

Never.

Shade stared at me from where he sat in a glass chair. No clear expression skittered across his face. "How are you feeling?"

"Outstanding." I looked at him and then turned to Toy. "In fact, that break with Nix was just what I needed."

"So you're not doing what you were doing anymore?" Toy asked without glancing at me.

"No. I'm not."

"Good," Shade said.

I wished I could have told him and the rest of the family right there that I was sorry I'd been doing quake and would never do it again. But that wasn't what they needed to hear. Most of them had no idea I'd been hooked on drugs. I figured I'd apologize to Shade and Toy later. But partly the real reason was that the urge to snort had rushed right back to me when I watched Nix walk away with Pappy.

"How's everybody been doing?" I asked.

All the kids shifted into a loud melody of stories and shrieks of delight. Somehow I gathered from their stories that we had a pool in the backyard, which was interesting—it hadn't been a part of the rental agreement. The twins believed the green neighbors next door were monsters. The triplets had apparently painted our baby sister green this morning in an effort to prove to the twins that green people weren't bad. Additionally, the boys wanted two more dogs due to the massive backyard and that Turtle seemed lonely and unhappy. Lastly, Mimi had her own bedroom, which she talked about with glee.

"Oh yeah, where's Nix? We saved two separate rooms for you and her." Mimi stood with a smile and pressed a remote control.

The table lit up in a white glow. The sides rose. The center of the table with the dishes lowered. A new metal surface slid out with a buzz and covered the open center. I had no idea where the dishes went or how they got there, but I knew that the table involved a dish washing process that eventually transported the plates—all clean and dry—to the kitchen cabinets through some elaborate tunnel system under the floor.

Thank the Duchess, Mimi knows all about this complicated tech shit.

"Nix'll be back this evening," I said to Mimi.

My dick twitched in my pants at the thought. I was getting tired of the effect she was having on me. Here she was far off somewhere in a bikini with a loser and had basically shoved me away, and still I craved her like no other.

"Are you sure you're not hungry?" Toy bounced my baby sister on his thigh. "Once you eat, we need to talk about that thing."

"What thing?" Mimi raised her eyebrows.

"The thing that is none of your business." Toy formed his face into a goofy expression.

"Fine. Keep your secrets." Mimi shrugged. "You'll need me to do something for you and then you'll have to tell me."

"Yeah. Well, then you'll know when that time comes." Shade laughed and leaned his head to the side. "We've been here for several days, Epic. You've missed your first day of work. Ain gave his boss an excuse, but I don't think Ain has any faith in us."

I waved the comment away. "Ain always is jittery. Call him up. Tell him to come over so we can go over it again."

"And Nix?" Toy crossed his arms over his chest.

"What about her?"

"Is she still a part of this."

"Yes." I noticed was Mimi quiet and studying us, as if she were trying to decipher what we were talking about.

She knew we were doing something illegal here, but we wouldn't let her know what, where, when, or why. Her job was to transfer the currency into portable banks. And even that duty made me nervous. If life was perfect, Mimi would have nothing to do with it. But life shoveled out crap sometimes, and in those moments I had to clean it up or just deal with it. My nose itched. I scratched it, knowing it wouldn't be enough. I yearned for just one hit to tide me over until the meeting.

"You straight, man?" Shade asked.

"I'm fine." I rubbed my face, headed out of the dining room, and switched my thoughts from quake to Nix. "I need to take a shower. Don't forget to call Ain."

"I will," Shade called back.

Ain was my cousin. He served as the key to getting Nix and me in the club. I had to make sure we stood face to face with him, guaranteeing that he would play his part with no problem. I also wanted to make sure the club still had the same security system and nothing more complex. There couldn't be any problems or mishaps. The stakes soared high for me, my family, and even Nix.

Nix. Fuck.

The damn woman's name incited tremors through my body. I loved pushing my dick inside her. The tip had slipped in between those plump lips with ease. The walls of her pussy formed around me—tight, wet, warm, and inviting. *Damn the Duchess.* It was paradise to slip in and out of her. My length glistened with her heated moistness. The rim of my head swelled with an intense need as it glided back and forth. I could have died right there with no regrets.

Her scent lingered far after I'd come inside of her and slowly pulled out. If we hadn't been in the restaurant, I would have asked to spill my cum all over those lush lips. I wanted to pump the head and watch the semen spurt all over that gorgeous face. I could imagine her licking the tip and sucking me dry. And the worst thing about the whole situation was that I yearned to be inside her in that moment soon after I came and any other instance after that. I desired her nonstop. *Damn you, Nix.* I grabbed my dick and increased my pace to the back where I spotted a staircase.

"You sure you don't want nothing to eat or drink?" Mimi yelled.

"I'm fine." I knew what I craved and it wasn't food or liquid. It was Nix's naked body moving above me as she rode my dick with no mercy. I knew if she ever climbed on top, she'd make me crumble into pieces. She had a talent with the way she rocked those hips and surely that luscious cunt of hers possessed some sort of magic or charge that floored the average man in seconds.

Dear God. I'll never get the taste of her pussy out of my head.

By the time I took my shower and calmed myself down, the kids had gathered around the television wall in the living room and my cousin Ain sat at the table with four women and several bottles of wine. Cartoons blasted around the area.

"Turn the TV down!" I yelled.

"Okay," the triplets called back in unison.

"Epic. I finally see you. Where in the darkness have you been, man?" Ain had a bald head and only reached my shoulder. He was around Mimi's height. She loved to remind him of that whenever she could. He wore some weird jacket and pants suit that boasted a crinkly gold material.

I couldn't believe he'd invited a bunch of women to my house while we were supposed to go over the hit. Or maybe I was more annoyed that he'd brought over women, ones with perky breasts and slim waists, long hair, and enchanting scents that made me gaze at them longer than I should. It wasn't like I couldn't ogle them. Nix had no claim to me, even though I'd tried my best to give it to her. But I was done with women for a while, at least until the hit resulted in success. Nix already clouded my brain with confusion. I didn't need another evil temptress in my life.

"Who are your friends?" I asked.

"I bet you want to know." Ain banged the table and laughed.

Shade already had his arm around one with a curly afro, brown complexion, and a slender frame. It was his type. Toy drooled in the corner, staring at the other women and looking like he was scared to approach them.

"Glad to see you." Ain rose and hugged me. "You see, ladies. I told you this bastard was big."

The blonde closest to him giggled.

"This is Sunset, Ice, Vicky, and Candy." Ain gestured to all the women. "They work at the club."

"Hello." I motioned for Ain to leave the living room with me. "Come over here for a minute."

"What's up?" Ain trailed behind me.

I waited until we got farther enough into the hallway. "Why would you bring strippers to a meeting where we are going to discuss robbing their strip club?"

"No. No." He waved his hands. "The girls are for after our talk. I can ask them to go in the living room."

I shook my head. "I have enough shit around the kids. I don't need to add half-naked women to the list. Let them hang out by the pool in the backyard."

"I like that idea. Maybe they'll be tempted to take off their clothes, huh?" He hit my chest.

I pushed his hand away. "Yeah. Maybe. Just get them out of here."

We walked back into the dining room. My body froze. Nix stood by the table, glaring at the women. She formed her hands into tight fists. It was almost comical that she would think that these women were competition, if not for the fact she'd pushed me away.

"Ladies. My cousins and I have something really important to talk about," Ain said. "Why don't you all go out back to the pool and we'll meet you soon. Feel free to take off those clothes and take a dip."

"Keep your clothes on." I dug my hands into my pockets. "At least until the kids go to sleep."

"When is that?" the girl with the afro licked her lips.

"In an hour." Shade patted her behind right before she escaped.

"And will I get to learn why people call you Epic?" the blonde asked as she stood. Her large breasts pressed against her corset. Her hard nipples poked through the material. The leather must have been thinner than most. It was difficult to look away as she stepped right in front of me and slipped her fingers across my chest. "Do they call you Epic because of your tall height and huge muscles or is it for what lays inside of your pants?"

I backed up and grinned. "That's my secret."

The blonde poked out her full lips and pouted. "What can I do to unlock it?"

Nix snarled from where she stood. The noise sounded loud and deadly. Everyone turned her way. Toy chuckled from the side.

"Who's this?" Ain raised his eyebrows.

"She's helping us out," I said. "I'll introduce you once the ladies go outside."

All the girls left except for the blonde. "Why does she get to stay?"

I began to say something, but Nix interrupted me, "Baby girl, you don't even have the right to ask. Now get the fuck out of here before I load you full of siphons."

The blonde huffed and placed her hands on her hips. "How rude—"

"Please go to the pool." I put my hand on her back and guided her out of the dining area. "I don't want any fighting around my brothers and sisters."

Nix centered her gaze on my hand. Once the blonde left and my hand went back to my side, Nix shifted her view to my face and scowled.

I mouthed the word *what*. Surly, she didn't think that she could tell me to fuck off and then turn around and expect me to never talk to other women again. Not that I planned on messing with the blonde, but there was no need for her to be pissed.

"Who invited the sluts?" She rolled her eyes and sat down.

"I did." Ain took his own chair. "What's your part in the hit?"

"Who are you again?" She twisted her lips in disgust.

"I'm the cousin with all the connections here." Ain turned his face to me and pointed at Nix. "So she's going to dance?"

"I can speak for myself. If you have questions, then ask me," Nix hissed.

"It doesn't look like you have any customer service." Ain laughed. "In fact, you scare the shit out of me."

"Good." She leaned back in her glass chair.

"If we need a dancer, then I got one that we can use," Ain offered.

"No way. She's perfect for the job." I faced Ain. "She has a nice body and can dance."

"Let me see." Ain threaded his fingers together. "Let's me and her go upstairs so she can show me why I should be so impressed like you are."

My hand itched to punch him. "No. She doesn't audition or go off anywhere with you."

"I said I can speak for myself." She glared at me.

"Yet, the answer is still no. Besides, let's all of us move on to the plan." *Before I get pissed.* "She stays on the job, Ain. That's not even a choice that you have in the matter. You're getting us inside the club and that's it. We're doing the hard part."

"Cool." Ain reached inside his jacket, pulled out a thin screen, and placed it on the table. "I have what you asked me for—a full layout of the club."

He pressed the black screen. A beep sounded. The whole display lit up to a bright blue. White lines formed around into boxes. White words labeled each section. Ain pressed a green button in the corner. Symbols and colors bled through the black screen and scattered across the map.

"This is the whole club. When we're done talking about our plan, you can keep this. I have another one at the house." Ain pushed the monitor to the center of the table as everyone leaned forward to get a better look. "All of the areas with yellow lines are the entrances. Green spots are the dance floors. Red is the rooms where they have sex."

"Do all of the dancers have sex?" Nix asked.

"No. It's just a small amount of humans that actually give up their pussy, but all of the androids can be taken into the back." Ain cleared his throat and continued gesturing to the screen. "The black rectangles are the bars. The violet circles are the bathrooms."

"None of this is sinking through, man." I let out an exasperated breath. "Do you have a legend for the map? There's no way I'm going to memorize the whole thing just from you talking about it."

"Oh, sure." He slid his thumb against the edge. A legend popped up on the right side of the screen, defining every area and what each symbol meant. We all stared at the layout for several minutes. Shade tapped his thumb against the table. I knew what that meant. He was designing the fastest way to get in and out.

Ain looked up at me. "What do you think so far, Epic?"

"I'd have to study the map some more and get a good walk through of the club." I combed my fingers through my hair. "It would take a week to check it out. I know we planned the end of this week, but I had no idea the club was this big."

"That's too long." Ain frowned.

"We could split the work." Nix touched the back rooms where the dancers' dressing areas were located. The region brightened. "I'll take this area. You can get the rest. That could speed everything up."

"And what do you need us to do?" Toy asked.

"I want you to know everything there is to know about the outer region. We need to have three aerial cars parked in different areas that we can escape to." I slid my index finger along the border of the club. "Ain, can you get all of the names and any information on the bouncers?"

Ain nodded.

"I'm talking anything that would give us an indication that they know how to fight and can shoot a gun. Their resumes should tell us enough. Once you have that, give it to Shade."

"If you can't get their resumes, then just give me their names. I'll do all the background research." Shade pointed to the white circles. "We could probably hide some extra weapons in the women's bathroom."

"There's an armored robot that does its rounds in the ladies' area at the beginning of each hour." Ain shrugged. "But I don't know if it has weapon sensors. The robot mainly goes in there to make sure none of the girls are doing drugs."

"Then I'll have to test it," Nix said. "I could slip a small gun in, place it in a vent inside the bathroom, and see what happens."

"Make sure you let me know when you do it so that I can watch your back." I avoided looking at her and kept my view on the map. "I want you safe."

"I'll do it the first day," she said.

"That's risky." Ain shook his head.

"Risky is exactly how I like it." She flashed him a wicked grin.

"Still," I centered my eyes on Nix to let her know I was serious, "make sure I'm aware when you're back there planting guns."

She mock saluted. "I won't forget."

"Toy and I will come inside and pretend like we're regular customers," Shade said.

"Stay focused on the job, not the ladies." I motioned to Toy since he was known to botch up a job due to drooling at jiggling bare tits.

"You're clean and now you're on my ass." He showed me his middle finger, but I knew it was all in good fun.

"What does he mean 'you're clean'?" Ain raised those eyebrows again.

"Nothing." I rose from my chair. Everyone else followed. I pressed the button to shut off the screen. "Okay. Tomorrow's the first day. Nix will plant the gun and see if any alarm is triggered. Ain will grab the guards' information for

Shade to check out. Toy, you search the outside. Everybody know what they need to do?"

They nodded.

"Then I guess we're done for now." I shrugged.

"Now let's check out these sexy ladies." Toy clapped his hands. I laughed as Shade pushed Toy out of the way and charged for the back. "No fair, Shade. No fucking fair!"

"Are they still fighting over women?" Ain walked out.

"Yep," I called back.

"Epic." Nix remained standing a few feet across from me. "We need to talk. Now."

"About what?"

She tapped her feet and lowered her lips into a frown. "About your . . . guests and why they're here."

"My guests?"

"The sluts."

"You think they're for me?"

"I can count, Epic. Four ladies for four guys."

"Shade is pretty lucky with women. He tends to get two or more to follow him to his bed." I leaned back on the wall across from her. "He's also really stingy too. He's only shared with me once and it was my birthday."

She rolled her eyes. "Regardless, what are your plans for this evening?"

Why do you even care? You rushed out with that mustache-wearing loser whale a minute after you came on my dick. All those words balanced on the tip of my tongue, but I held them in. Instead, I zoomed my eyes in and drank in her image—olive cleavage spilled out of her corset, her full lips poked out in my direction, and damn, those soft fingers knew how to grab my dick in just the perfect way.

She bit her lip and had to know I was relishing in her sexiness. "Are you going to answer me?"

"I don't have any plans. I'm just going to put the kids to sleep and then lounge by the pool." I twisted away and headed off.

"Epic. Wait."

I paused.

Do I even want to know what else she wants to discuss?

In one moment she made me come, either from her touching my flesh or ordering me to touch myself. In the next instance, she pushed me away and claimed there was nothing between us. Seeing the club's layout screen pushed me back into the momentum of the hit, the real reason why I stood in this house with my family sitting in the room next door. I was here for a job, to rob lots of money that could change my brothers' and sisters' lives. I'd already wasted precious days we didn't have from my recovery of quake.

"What do want, Nix?" I couldn't waste any more seconds by sniffing after her. I faced her one last time.

"I'd rather you not hang out by the pool tonight."

"Really?"

"Yes. That's what I want."

"Interesting. You know what I want from you, right?" I dug my hands into my pockets.

She averted her eyes for a few seconds and then looked back at me. They seemed strained. "Yeah, and I can't give you that."

"Then we don't need to talk about what we want anymore. We just need to leave each other alone and move on. Just keep the hit on your mind and don't worry about what I'm doing this evening."

Her mouth dropped open. She quickly recovered and asked, "Move on?"

"We remain business partners."

"Okay."

"Good."

"Are you planning on fucking that blonde or any of those other women?" Rage glazed over her eyes.

"Did you fuck Pappy?"

"No."

"Then I'll go to my room alone tonight."

She bit her lip again. I hated it. That plump skin should have been between my teeth.

"And will you be going to your room alone tomorrow?"

"I don't know yet. Why does it even matter to you?"

"I don't know why."

"I'm surprised you care."

"Me too," she muttered.

Silence moved between us for several seconds. What could I do? She'd experienced the darkest side of an evil man, the part that desired to hurt, torture, and imprison her. And yet she survived. She'd risen out of the pain when many would have given up and taken their life. She kept living and moving forward.

I hungered for her so hard that it rocked my body when she was in the room and my dick throbbed anytime I heard her name. She was intoxicating and I needed to be clean from her before I shifted into a dark man similar to the guy who hurt her. Because deep within the secret corners of my head, I ached to make her mine, to stop waiting patiently on the side and force her into my will. And if I did and won, she wouldn't survive, so I had to walk away.

Someone has to stop it now before it goes too far.

"I'm becoming addicted to you." I narrowed my eyes at her. "And I'm losing control."

She edged back. Maybe it was due to fear, disgust, or just instinct.

"I can't be that evil bastard that hurts and tries to jail you. I won't let myself go that far." I exhaled. "And I don't think I can have you like I dream."

"What's your dream?"

"You near me every second of the day. Your body formed against mine at night as we sleep, so much that your scent sinks in my bed sheets." I advanced her way without meaning to. "I long to taste your skin when I'm hungry for you, which right now is anytime I'm awake."

"I can't—I just can't."

"I understand."

"What about what you said in the hallway of that restaurant, that I owned you?"

"You do," I whispered.

"Then no other women." She scowled.

I grinned and tilted my head to the side. "You own me, but you'll have to give me a reason to not use another woman to get you off of my mind. You'll have to be in my bed."

"But, Epic, I just can't—"

I held my hands up. "I know. You can't and that's okay, but I can't follow you around, sniffing and begging either, because eventually I'll lose full control and do the things I want to do when I see another man next to you, whispering in your hair and touching your hand. I'll kill him."

She stared at the ground. "Then we're just business partners."

"Exactly."

She said nothing else.

"Goodnight, Nix." I walked out, rushed upstairs, and headed to the bathroom inside my bedroom to take another shower, a cold one to keep me sane through the night as I thought about her laying in her bedroom a few doors down.

Did I make a mistake?

I should have just shut up and tried to fuck her or even worse, gone downstairs, ran outside, and took the blonde to my bed. *No. Bad idea.* Nix wasn't the type of female you played those games with, and even though my sexing the blonde wouldn't have been some sort of retaliation against Nix, I had a feeling that Nix would hurt the blonde and me. It was best to keep women out of my bed for a few days. Maybe at the end of the week our minds would be clear of each other and things would return to normal.

I stepped out of the shower and headed to my room with a towel wrapped around my waist. Darkness draped my bedroom. *I thought I had the lights on?* A figure lay in my bed.

"Who's that?" I asked.

"If you're going to sleep in bed with me, then you'll have to put on some shorts." Nix kept her back to me.

"This is my room and bed."

"You want me to leave?"

"No."

"Then put on some shorts."

I smiled. "That's the only rule?"

"No sex, kissing, saying things like you love me, or reciting poems."

"Fuck. I'm actually pissed about the poetry restriction."

"We're just sleeping together in the same bed."

"As what?"

"Business partners."

I licked my lips, imagining what she wore under that sheet. "That's it?"

"Yep, just business partners."

"And tomorrow night?"

"We'll still just be business partners."

"But will you be in my bed tomorrow night?"

She sighed. "We'll see."

CHAPTER 14
PHOENIX

The moons' light seeped into Epic's bedroom, casting long eerie shadows across the floor and walls that resembled stretched-out arms and hands. They made me feel caged in and trapped, like their murky fingers were attempting to hold me down beside Epic's sleeping form. I was finding it harder and harder to breathe. And that pissed me off.

I'm colossally stupid.

There's really no other explanation for why I would come to *sleep* in Epic's bed with him. I keep claiming I don't want more from him, that I can't handle it, and yet . . . here I am. Like a friggin' virgin on prom night getting a hotel room with her long-term boyfriend, and still claiming she might not have sex with him. *Yeah, right.* I flopped over onto my back and huffed. The thought of Epic with one of those girls boiled my blood. At least this way I knew who he was with and what he was doing.

Although I shouldn't care—but I do care—but I can't care—FUCK!

"You're huffing a lot over there. What's wrong? Can't sleep?" Epic's muscled arm snaked out and pulled me into his side. "There are a few things I could do to help you with that."

Isn't that part of the problem?

I tensed. "No, I'm good."

Epic snorted but didn't say anything else.

I blinked into the darkness. "Epic?"

"Yeah?"

"Why do you have artificial eyes?"

"I'm surprised it took you so long to ask. That's usually the first thing people seem to want to know."

"Yeah, well, I've had other things on my mind and we've been busy."

He laughed. The deep rumble swept across my skin and soothed my ragged nerves. "You know those warning labels on the back of cleaning bots right next to the tubes near the arms? Sometimes they're real tiny and long."

"Mmmm-hmmm."

He laughed again in response to some inside joke that only he heard. "And most of the time on the bots there are these huge warning labels in bright blue that say something like, 'Do not pull out liquid sourcing tubes unless wearing safety goggles.'"

"Yes." I hit his chest. "Would you just tell me what happened?"

"Well, I'm the reason why that label exists. I'm the first dumbass that wrenched the tubes out."

"What? You must be joking, right?"

"No. I'd never joke with you like that, Nixie baby." He pressed his lips against my forehead and inhaled my scent.

"When I was a kid, around five years old, I was just messing around by myself. I yanked the tubes out just to see what would happen. The stuff those robots use sprayed into my eyes. I mean I think that stuff is full of lye or ammonia, flesh-burning chemicals. Either way, it burned the shit out of my cornea. I sat in the hospital for days filled with hope that I'd get to see soon. I was too young and figured everything just worked out always, until the doctor said I'd be permanently blind."

Sympathy filled me as I imagined the young Epic waiting for news about his damaged eyes. "How long were you blind?"

"A year. During that whole time my parents sued the company that made the robots. I guess the case had a human judge, because he ruled against the company, forced them to pay for surgery to give me artificial eyes, and hand over a decent-sized settlement that lasted my family for a several years."

"Do you still remember what it was like to be blind?"

Minutes of quiet passed and then he finally answered, "Yes. I'm lucky my parents got on the case because I don't think I would have did all the things I've done in my life without these eyes. Although, my mom did teach me how to play guitar the whole time I was blind, to lift my spirits."

"That's right. You said you performed in a band."

"Chameleon."

"*The* Chameleon?" I climbed out of his arms and sat up. "Holy Duchess of Light. They did have another lead singer back in the day, but his bald head was covered in tattoos."

Epic brightened his eyes, illuminating the room. He parted his thick hair. Electric ink glittered in the light.

"The tats are still there. I let my hair grow out for my mom when I stopped performing with the band to take care of her. She loved my hair."

He pulled me back down to him, his eyes dimmed back to normal. Darkness blanketed us in an intimate cocoon. I ran my fingers through his hair, relishing its softness. "I kind of like your hair too. So what happened to your parents? They sound like they were really caring people."

"They're both dead."

"I'm so sorry, Epic."

"No. Don't be." He brushed his fingertips against my skin. Shivers branched out from every place he touched. "My mother died from a rare blood disease. It didn't happen all of a sudden. We all had time to say goodbye to her. My dad died soon after, from . . . I guess you can say 'a broken heart.'"

"That's so sad."

"It is, but I bet they're together now. They loved each other so much." He sighed. "I remember watching them and hoping that I'd have just some of what they had, just a lady that loved me half as much as Mom loved Dad."

I bit my lip, unprepared to push further on the topic. He, in not so many words, told me what he really wanted from me, and I couldn't be that for him. Teddy had burned, beaten, and tortured all that kind of love out of my heart.

"Mom would have loved you if she had met you," he said.

"I really doubt she would have been all that thrilled to have an ex-stripper con-artist slash robber as a daughter-in-law."

"You forget that she's my mom. Does it look like Shade, Toy, and I were raised by some virginal, pure goddess?"

I snorted.

"Mom had a rough life. She did a lot of things she didn't want to just to survive, just to put food on our table. She had plenty of secrets in her past that she never wanted to discuss, and I never pushed it." He gazed into my eyes. "You remind me of her so much. She had this hard, prickly outer shell around her that was almost impossible to break through, but when you did, love poured out to reward you. She was also there when you needed her, like what you did for me in my darkest times.

"It was only business." I averted my eyes.

"Nevertheless, she always said I needed a no-nonsense woman to keep my attention."

Silence thickened the air. I was glad he'd left it alone. I just wasn't that woman. I wasn't like his mom. I was just Phoenix—disappointed daughter, runaway, stripper, murderer, whale fisher, and thief. I didn't do relationships anymore. I did things for myself and no one else. Sure I'd only become selfish out of necessity—because I'd discovered that if I didn't take care of myself, then no one else would—but I was selfish all the same.

The one person that had claimed to love and want to take care of me had left me badly burned . . . quite literally. I could only truly trust myself. No one would be getting past my hard, prickly outer shell—as Epic had described it. *Then why am I laying in this bed with him?* Thoughts of Epic and me swirled around in my head. I bit my bottom lip until a tiny dot of blood landed on my tongue.

"Why do you want me so much? You hardly know me." I really hated how vulnerable and small my voice sounded.

"Besides everything that I've already said? In the end, there's just something about you and—I guess the heart wants what the heart wants. There's no point in arguing with it." He pulled me closer and nuzzled my neck. I could feel his smile against my suddenly overheated skin. "Why do you ask, Nixie baby? You're not thinking about leaving this bed, are you? Because I'm not letting you go."

A grin stretched across my face and I hated myself for loving his possessiveness of me. "I don't know why I asked. I guess I was just wondering."

Minutes of quiet flew by with neither of us needing to say another word as we lay in each other's arms. Epic's breathing started to even out again, letting me know he was falling back asleep. But something nagged in the back of my mind and it wouldn't allow me peace enough to join Epic in slumber.

"Epic?" I said his name again as I ran my hands through his silky hair. I think if he was a cat, he would have purred.

"Yeah, Nixie baby?"

"Nothing, never mind." *God, why am I acting like a lovesick teenager in the darkness?* I wasn't one to get tongue tied and to seek comfort in any way—especially in a man's arms. *Yet here I am.*

"Are we going to stay up all night and have one of those talks? You know the ones you always see in movies and shit—about all of our feelings and rainbows and bunnies?" Epic chuckled before nipping at the skin just below my ear. I shivered.

"Don't be ridiculous."

"Yeah, okay. Something is going on in that sexy head of yours." Epic propped himself up on his elbow and gazed down at me, his eyes illuminated in the dark. "What did he do to you? Besides torture you? Not that that isn't enough— it's just—well, it seems like more somehow."

"He broke me," I whispered.

Epic ran a finger down the side of my face. "No Nixie baby, he hurt you, but you're too strong to be broken. No one could ever break you."

"You're wrong." Silent tears spilled down my cheeks. "I'll never be able to trust a man again. Not the way I want anyway. And love, I'll never find the kind of love I want. He broke that part of me too. Sure, I survived, but he stole something—I'm not even sure what—but it's gone for good." I took in huge breath and exhaled, trying to calm myself.

"No, I don't believe that," Epic murmured. "You wouldn't be here right now if that was all true."

"You don't know that. I don't even know why I'm here."

He left a trail of soft, wet kisses across my cheek. "You can trust me. Tell me what I need to do to prove it to you. I'll do anything. I'll be your anything. Just tell me what to do and I'll spend the rest of my life giving you a better life."

"I-I don't know." Maybe he was right. Would I even still be capable of wanting those things if I was completely broken? I just wasn't sure anymore. "I wish I could—I want to trust you, but I—"

"You can." Epic sat up and pulled a thin metal chain from around his neck. On it was what appeared to be a small charm that formed into a heart. I'd asked him earlier if he had a picture in it and he said that he didn't. He gently slipped the chain over my head.

"This is beautiful. What is it?" I guess he hadn't lied about the picture; otherwise he wouldn't be giving it to me. I inspected the charm in the dim lighting that spilled through the windows from the moons.

Carved letters etched into the back of it and spelled out his name. I ran my fingers over it. A buzzing noise emitted from the locket before the heart popped open and light poured out of it. An illuminated screen rose up in front of us. A bright green line horizontally traveled across the screen in a pattern of waves and beeps. Colored dots sat on the side. Some of the labels said mitral valve, tricuspid valve, aortic valve, pulmonary valve, defibrillator, and other words I didn't understand.

Is this a heart key?

I'd heard about the technology, but I'd never actually seen one and barely knew much about it. A heart key was used to upload all information about a person's heart into a special piece of equipment that doctors used to operate with nanotechnology. It meant that Epic had some kind of heart condition. If something went wrong and he didn't have the key to give to doctors, it spelled almost certain death.

Or maybe this is something else.

"Press the button that says pulmonary valve," Epic said.

I raised my hand and touched the thin air near the section. It warmed my fingertips. The screen shifted to an all-black image. A reddish-orange, oval-shaped image compressed and relaxed over and over in a matter of seconds, never stopping.

"This is my heart." He pointed to the center of the image. "It's hard to tell since my heart isn't next to a normal one, but my pulmonary valve is smaller than the average human's. I used to have lots of heart attacks as a kid." A chuckle escaped his lips. "I guess I really gave my parents a hard time during my childhood. Either we were in the hospital for my eyes or we returned for my heart."

"So this is like a heart monitor for you?" My own heart pounded.

He put it around my neck? Why?

"Monitoring my heart is one of its duties. It does a lot of things, but most importantly—if I have a heart attack . . ." He waved his hand around the screen. The original view returned. He pointed to the bottom where it showed an image of a yellow key. "If I get chest pains or any other indicator of an oncoming heart attack, then I press this key and it does its magic."

I tried to lift it back over my head to give it to him.

"No." He formed his lips into a straight line. "You keep it. I love the idea of you wearing the key to my heart."

"What?" My mouth dropped open with shock. "No, no, no, no—No! I can't—No!"

Is he completely insane?

"You now hold my heart in your hands—almost literally."

"You're crazy—fucking insane. I'm holding your life in my hands. Do you really get that? You just gave me the power over your life and you practically just met me." I licked my lips nervously. "I can't."

Epic grinned. "Aw, Nixie baby, does that mean you care? It's just a valve thing—nothing serious. I haven't had to use that thing for almost ten years now."

I stared up at Epic's expectant face. Why had he given me the key? Why did he want me? *Does it really matter?* He just gave himself to me. I literally owned him. Something inside of me broke. I mean—fuck—the man just gave me a literal key to his heart.

"Kiss me," I demanded hoarsely.

Without hesitation, Epic complied. His lips came down almost brutally on top of mine and his tongue pushed into my mouth, completely dominating me. And I let him. I let him take control as he tore my tiny shorts and tank from my body. I spread my legs open wide, moist and so ready for him.

"I can never get enough of you." He dipped his fingers into my wet pussy and groaned.

A blistering need set my whole body on fire. "Stop talking and fuck me."

He pushed inside of me roughly, with no mercy, and I delighted in the feel of his hard cock. There was some kind of weird dynamic, one that my Epic-befuddled brain was hard pressed to sort out at the moment. And although he ruled over me with that huge body wrapped in muscle and power, I still felt in control. A slapping sound ensued, and his grunts echoed my cries of bliss.

I'd never felt anything like it before.

Epic rolled me over. I rode him at my own pace, rolling my hips ruthlessly and sliding up and down on him as he cupped my breasts and pinched my swollen nipples. My pussy clamped on to him, so hot and soaking with desire. I stared into his lust-filled eyes as he watched me bring us both pleasure. He mumbled incoherent and yet sweet-sounding gibberish that had my heart swelling inside my chest even as I rocked my way toward my release.

Are we making love? Is that what we're doing? Am I falling for him? Questions swirled around in my brain that I couldn't answer, so instead of pondering them anymore, I threw my head back and screamed. My orgasm spread through my body like wild fire. My vision darkened around the edges.

The next thing I knew Epic flipped me over onto my back. I shrieked in surprise.

"Fuck. I'm almost there." He yanked his cock out and fisted the tip. "I need to paint you with me."

Inch by inch, I dragged my tongue along the bottom of my lip, knowing that he was on the edge of pleasure and insanity. "You want to come all over me, baby?"

He trembled above me. His arm shook as he tried with all his might not to move his hand over the tip of his dick and come. "F-fuck yeah. Can I?"

"Beg me."

"Please." His body quaked for a second, but he gained control of himself. "Please Nixie baby. Please!"

I grinned. "Come on me, baby. Do it now."

White-hot liquid burst out of his throbbing head and landed all over my face and breasts. Normally I would've found it insulting, but the way he painted me with his pleasure felt right somehow. He was claiming me, and I was letting him. I slid my hands over my body and rubbed it in like lotion.

"Fuck, that's hot." He groaned as his gaze followed my every movement. He snapped picture after picture. Light flashed so much around me I thought *I* would turn blind.

"Enough, Epic."

"Sorry. I just don't ever want to forget this moment. When I'm at my worst, I'll pull these images out of my head and think of you."

I lifted a finger to my lips and tasted his sweet release. "Mmmm . . . you taste good." I knew my smile was anything but demure. "I think I need a shower now."

Epic grinned. "No, *we* need a shower now. I'm going to clean you all up, just to do it all over again."

"How can you already be ready again?"

"Because that's what you do to me, Nixie baby."

I bit my cheek and suppressed my smile. "I'm not going to be able to walk tomorrow, am I?"

"I don't think either of us will." Epic scooped me up and threw me over his shoulder, heading toward the shower.

We made love in the shower for so long and so loud that Toy stomped in and demanded we shut up—but of course we didn't. And Epic wasn't satisfied until we both collapsed, completely spent, just as morning light began to spill through his bedroom window, replacing the moons' shadows with the illumination of new beginnings.

CHAPTER 15
EPIC

After the breakthrough between Nix and me last night, this morning I woke up, got a little crazy, and splurged by buying us both matching aerial scooters. A fire pattern covered hers. Black guitars decorated mine. Shade would trip if he knew. Luckily, he'd been too busy with the kids, the women that Ain had brought over, and the orders I gave him for the hit.

Nix and I rode the scooters to Dynamics. I'd made sure we took the long way so the whole path was clear of other drivers. Ain called earlier and told me that he got Nix an audition with the head managers. I was supposed to start work as a bouncer that night, but I decided to come early and make sure those managers kept their filthy hands to the side when Nix began to rock those hips.

We flew away from the city. Multi-colored glass towers shifted to scattered towns with hills of thick grass and machine-operated farms that sprayed pink liquid over black soil. The trail I guided us on was called a Free Path. Like most planets in the galaxy, areas with large poles that bore a yellow flag symbolized that all aerials could rush through without following the usual highway laws. Free Paths existed outside of major cities and over oceans and deserted areas.

"Damn the Duchess! This thing moves!" Nix's silk dress wavered in the breeze.

Her midnight-black stands danced in the air as she sped past me. Violet shades wrapped around her face. She'd refused to wear the helmet I bought her. Not that a helmet could save her from a hundred-foot fall, but it would have made me less jittery. She had her back exposed today. The dress tied around her and exposed the huge Phoenix as it flew out of the flames. For a few seconds I imagined the Phoenix flew to me.

"I just have to test this baby out." Her scooter exploded with speed. She zipped by. A line of smoke trailed behind her.

I put my black sunglasses on and yanked the dial back on my scooter. Red lights glowed on the dashboard as I increased the speed to catch up with her. "You promised, Nix!"

"Going seventy miles per hour sucks!"

A gust of wind blew past me. My shirt and jeans rippled. "A hundred fifty miles per hour is deadly. Slow the fuck down!"

I'm sure she groaned, but I couldn't hear her. Her scooter rang out several beeps. The yellow lights at the back of her vehicle flashed to signal to the riders behind that she would be stopping. She slowed down and I adjusted my speed with her. She was lucky this was the free path where no trafficbots monitored the area or she would have been captured, ticketed, and maybe even had her vehicle towed away.

She drove to my side. "You're acting like you're my father. In case it's not obvious, that's not a good thing."

"Fuck it. I don't want anything to happen to you." I gripped the handles on my scooter hard. *Holy Duchess, please don't let anything happen to her. I can't take any more losses.* "We have twenty more miles before the sector of Lady Polynesia comes up and less than a mile after that for the club. Let's get there in one piece, Nixie baby."

"Nah, I don't want to." She stuck out her tongue and zoomed off, honking her horn.

I'm going to strangle her, right after I fuck the shit out of her. Maybe I'll bend her over and take her right in the ass, right on that scooter that I'm going to destroy.

"Worst case scenario, I can swim!"

"You're insane," I yelled back.

"Says the guy that gave me his heart key!"

I couldn't help but grin.

Yeah. I am a little more insane than her. But who else deserved to wear it? Who else would ever deserve to wear it? She is my match in every way possible.

I'd been slowly dying from my snorting quake when she entered my life and saved me. Only the Duchess of Light knows what would have happened to me if I'd remained on the drug. I could have been a danger to my little brothers and sisters. Nix didn't know me. She said she helped me due to business reasons, but I knew better. She was falling for me as hard and fast as I was falling for her. Therefore, my heart key rested around the right neck. I couldn't think of anyone more worthy than her.

"Let's race!" Nix glanced over her shoulders.

"Let's do something even more fun."

"What?"

"Look forward to where you are driving and do it at a safer speed."

"Boring!" She increased her speed. I rushed after her.

Nothing but ocean lay underneath us. It was clear blue and reflected the rays of the sun. A few steel boats cruised under and cast out metal nets. I didn't see any humans on the deck and assumed the whole fishing unit was run by robots or some sort of remote control where a staff manipulated it at a surface station. That's how fishing was done back on earth. The robots had dominated the fishing and farming industry. The only people who grew things were enthusiasts who had the land to plant a few vegetable seeds. "You're fucking insane!"

"Insanely fun! Epic, watch this!" She rose five feet up. I lifted my head as she twirled the scooter and her around in one swift moment.

"Nix, I'm going to kill you!" My nerves flared on edge.

"You'll have to catch me first." Clouds of smoke burst in the air as she raced away.

At first I began to scream curses at her, but then I watched her bob her head like her own special music played in her head. I'd never seen her this way, so carefree and relaxed. I loved it.

So I shoved my stress down and did something even crazier . . . I just laughed. It bubbled out of me.

"Catch you, huh?" I chased her, yanking the dial on the scooter all the way down. The metal on my display shook.

The engine hummed. My teeth chattered. I unbuckled my pants and opened them. My jeans fell to my ankles. I shoved down my boxer briefs. Cool air tickled my skin. My dick lay limp between my legs.

"Catch this!" My scooter whizzed past as I wiggled my ass at her. Laughter exploded behind me. Even over the humming of my engine, I could hear her hooting with joy.

Less than twenty minutes later we arrived in the sector of Lady Polynesia where club Dynamics was located. The sun had set on this side of the planet. Darkness painted the sky. The Free Path switched back into the aerial highway. Nix and I moved into line with the other floating scooters.

Music played from many of the Hoover crafts—popular pops songs I'd heard too many times about stars and love. It was funny how bands these days couldn't come up with a more innovative song topic than comparing their love to stars. Currently, the song "Star Gazer" hovered at number one on the charts and had been there for months. Number two was "Love Star", then "Stars of My Heart." Number four was the rap song "Star Fucker", although the radio version was "Star Lover." I groaned and wished I'd gotten the upgraded scooters with the ViFi Signals that captured sound waves from up to five planets.

Many of the buildings gleamed a shade of bright red and lit up the area around them. Most of them were restaurants and hotels. They extended high up into the sky and bordered the aerial highway on both sides. Although Lady Polynesia was the sector's official name, many referred to it as the Red Light District. I could see why. It was reminiscent of the red light districts on earth.

Perfume drifted to my nostrils. A copper platform floated my way. The vehicle must have been the size of a van. Five naked women stood on the top surface, holding the side bars. A man sat in the front and turned the wheel. The ladies whistled in my direction and wiggled their hips. Their nipples stood erect on those perky breasts. Upside down triangles of silky hair lay between their thick thighs.

White lights slid past the top of the machine. "Come play with us. All currencies accepted."

"You see something you like?" Anger laced Nix's voice.

I turned to Nix. A neutral expression spread across her face, but I knew she was pissed. I smirked. "There's nothing over there for me. I'm just looking."

She twisted her lips to the side as if she were thinking about it and then said, "Yeah, well, I guess looking is okay. Especially if you're only looking so that you can see how utterly lacking they all are in comparison to me."

"I'm glad you approve." I laughed.

Farther ahead, letters glittered in the sky and spelled out *Dynamics.* A massive building rested under the flying letters. All black glass covered it. Black glass tended to be the regulation now for strip clubs, brothels, casinos, and drug dens. There couldn't be any other color but black, to represent darkness and to signal that this place was a business where the Duchess of Light would never venture to. Apparently the Duchess as too pure for these establishments, but had no problem taxing these places to fuel the galaxy's economy. I hated how the Duchess looked down on them.

"Alright, Nixie baby. That's our stop." I gestured to the club and flipped on my right signal. Nix followed. We parked on the roof with all the other vehicles. Two bars zipped out of the sides of our scooters and wrapped around the ignition to keep them secure from any aerial jackers.

"That was fun." She gripped my ass and squeezed. "Do I get to see this again tonight?"

"After I see yours." I seized her curvaceous ass and pulled her into a kiss. We stood there for several minutes, sucking on our tongues, biting our lips, and slipping our hands across our bodies. I groaned and stepped back. "We have a job to do."

"I didn't forget." She blushed.

I nipped at her chin. "Then stop making me forget. According to our plan, you're supposed to be my cousin."

I scanned the parking lot, but luckily no one was around.

"Well, we're clearly kissing cousins." She strolled forward and approached the door before me. I hurried to the doorknob before she could grab it and opened it for her. She blushed again. "Who would have thought my kidnapper and master of chains would turn out to be a gentleman?"

I winked. "I try."

An electronic bass boomed below. I couldn't hear the song because we were so far up. Smoke lingered in the dark passageway. A light blinked on and off where it hung from the ceiling. One bald-headed guy stood inside. Small screens sank in the wall behind him. One screen displayed the parking lot.

Fuck. He may have seen our kiss. I hope it doesn't matter. We'll have to be more careful.

"Only employees enter the back." He held up his hand.

"I start as a bouncer tonight. She's interviewing."

"Welcome to Dynamics. Please show me your ID or scanners." He stood and reached my height.

"I don't have any scanners in my wrist." I pulled my identification out of my pocket and showed the one-inch disk to him. He slid a pen over it. My face, name, address, and planetary status showed up on the top screen.

"Epicaderous Brownstone?" Nix covered her mouth with her land, but still, I heard the giggling. The guy chuckled too.

"It's Epic." I shrugged. "Give me a break. My mom loved that cartoon *The Gods of Septors* when she was a little girl. Epicaderous was her favorite."

"I thought that was a three-legged dog?" The guy's face scrunched up into a confused look.

"No. He was the leader," I grumbled.

"So you're the new bouncer. Are you Ain's cousin?"

"Yeah." I motioned to Nix. "I came early to escort her to her audition. She's my cousin too."

"Good. The bosses don't let couples work together." He scanned Nix's ID and then pointed to the dimly lit staircase that lowered into the club. "The club is made up of five levels. The bosses are on the third. They'll be waiting for her by the center stage. Usually they have some gear for her to put on. I think you can pick it out and change in the bathrooms on the side."

"Sounds good." I got ready to walk down there with her.

He blocked my way. "No guys but the bosses are allowed during the audition. Not even relatives."

Then I don't want her to go.

I didn't like us being separated until I was more familiar with the club and the people who owned it. I almost dragged her out of there, but knew it would just piss her off. *Maybe I should keep her out of this hit and convince her to play a smaller role.* I glanced at her and she shrugged. As usual, no fear swam through those green eyes. A mask of confidence clamped on to her face. And in that instance, I remembered I couldn't keep Nix out of the plan no matter how much I desired to keep her safe. She made her own rules and only followed them, not mine or any others.

"You still want to do the audition?"

"Of course." She tossed me an odd look.

"Okay."

She grabbed my heart key that lay between her cleavage, outlined the edge of it with her thumb, and walked to the stairs. "Wish me luck, Epicaderous."

I'd remember that later when I had her legs spread across my bed.

CHAPTER 16

PHOENIX

Seriously? Had Epic really considered the idea that I might not still want to do the audition? Because what—he couldn't go with me?

Epic was turning out to be nothing like I thought he would be. Beneath his hard exterior was an intelligent, caring, loving, and sort of needy man. But damn, if his skills between the sheets and his magnificent body didn't make up for that one failing. Or even his heart, for that matter. By giving me his heart key last night he'd managed to slip into mine. Maybe I was insane like he said, but I was beginning to believe that a relationship between us might just be possible.

I made my way through the dimly lit club to the third floor. As soon as I stepped through the beaded doorway I saw two men leaning against a bar facing what was definitely center stage. I mean it was huge and smack-dab in the middle of the room.

Showtime! Oh joy!

I plastered on my best flirty smile and swung my hips with purpose. Both men's heads roamed openly over the curves of my body, but I didn't care. In this case, that was a good thing. They looked nothing like Epic. They must have been half his size, but both had muscular bodies that were showcased in their red plastic shirts. Mustaches rested above the top of their lips and curled up at the ends, just like Pappy's did. I supposed it must be the current style amongst a certain type of man—the type that liked to pay for their women. Neither of them had a chiseled face like Epic, but they didn't possess grotesque faces either—just kind of plain.

I stood directly in front of them. "Hi, I'm Nix. I'm here to audition. I was told you might have something for me to wear before we start?"

They both looked like they took decent care of themselves, but they were also complete skeezes. Being so close to them kind of made me feel a little nauseous. It was like I could read their lecherous thoughts about me on their douche bag faces.

"Nice to meet you, Nix," Tweedle Dee said as his much-too-bright teeth glinted in the lights. "There'll be two parts to the audition. First, we need to see what you can do on the main stage, and if you please us, visually speaking, then we get to test out your lap-dancing skills."

I narrowed my eyes as Tweedle Dum snickered, and yet I somehow managed to keep my smile in place. I was fairly certain that the lap dance portion of my audition had been a recent development. They'd probably added it as soon as I walked in the door.

I had a tendency to attract the worst kind of men, even in a place like this. "Yeah, sure, so what about the costume?"

Tweedle Dee spoke up again. "Just strip off what you're wearing. That'll be fine."

"Is this a fully nude club? I thought it was—"

"We're not going to waste the supplies such as pasties if you're not worth it. If we hire you, which depends on if you perform well today, then we'll provide you with a costume of our choosing."

I ground my teeth together. In a world like this; it was the survival of the fittest. And if I didn't put my foot down now, I might as well just lie down and spread my legs for both of them. I wasn't stupid. They were trying to see how far they could push me. They both were hoping I might be one of the clueless girls who walked into their club and thought everyone had to give them sexual favors in exchange for their job. I might not get the job, but I wasn't about to become a prostitute either.

"Not going to happen, boys." I smirked as Tweedle Dee and Tweedle Dum's faces both fell into identical frowns. "This isn't my first time to a show. I'll dance for you. You can look, but there isn't going to be any touching of any kind."

Tweedle Dee started to open his mouth, but I raised my hand abruptly to silence him. "And before you kick me out, I'd like to say one thing first. I may not be jonesing to be one of your probably many whores, but I can guarantee you that I'll make your club a lot of money. Now if you let me audition for you the proper way, I'll let you be the judge of my money-making skills and not my dick-sucking skills."

Both men stared at me in shock for a moment before Tweedle Dee broke the silence. "Alright. But you better be good or I'm having Joey throw you out of here head first."

I grinned with triumph. "Oh, I'll be good, baby. The best you've ever seen."

Tweedle Dee snorted. "Yeah, we'll see."

I made my way over to the stage and pulled myself up onto it, deciding not to bother entering from the back—it was pointless really. "So—music and lighting? Or am I just supposed to make do without them like the costume?"

Tweedle Dee made his way over to the empty DJ booth and climbed into it. "I'll give you some music, just to be fair." He chuckled to himself.

"Yeah, fair." I grumbled under my breath before smiling brightly up at him. "Alright, well, how about—"

Tweedle Dee waved his hand at me. "I didn't say you'd get to pick the music, just that you'd have some." Tweedle Dum laughed openly as I narrowed my eyes at Tweedle Dee. With a flick of his wrist, music suddenly began to blare from speakers that were placed around the club but out of view. *Nice.*

I took a moment to let the music begin to roll over me, to seep into my system through my pores. When I danced, I always let the music be my partner. It led me with a steady hand and told me exactly what to do. It never let me down.

A steady deep bass thumped, causing my pulse to beat in time with it. I rolled my neck and listened as the singer's hypnotic voice spoke directly to my soul.

"Every day I've tried to resurrect myself, from ashes of my life of yesterday, but each time's been a little harder trying to arise, that now I feel I'm really down to stay."

It was an early Chameleon song, and I immediately recognized the sultry tone as Epic's, now that I knew it so intimately. His voice was a thing of beauty and the pain that it held wound itself around my heart and squeezed. I began to move slowly, letting Epic's sweet tones caress my skin lovingly, which caused goose bumps to erupt across my flesh.

"Every day I've tried to re-invent myself, for who I think I am I cannot be, but as I metamorphosis and shed my painful past, I lose my too few friends and family."

Yes, I'd heard the song before, and I'd loved it, but I'd never really listened to the lyrics, like really listened. Of course what I knew now about Epic changed the meaning of the words for me, and sadness washed over me. He was so full of deep-seated emotional angst. I could only hope that one day I could heal him the way he was slowly beginning to heal me. It was in that moment that I decided I'd spend the rest of my life trying.

I gyrated slowly as I let my dress slip from my body, my nipples were tight little buds as I pictured myself dancing for Epic in a room all by ourselves as he sang his heart-wrenching song for me and me alone. Suddenly the chorus broke out and I followed my urge to grip the pole in the center of the stage. I began to swing around, doing various acts of aerial gymnastics.

"I can't seeeee—What will beeee-come of me?"

Epic's voice screeched with pain as I danced for him. Because that's what I was doing, I was dancing for him, and I'd never stop. The chorus dropped off and the music flowed back into the slower melody of another verse.

"Every day I've tried to repossess myself, from overwhelming anger in my soul, but though there's light at tunnel's

end, it's so damn far away, that now I feel I'll never reach
that goal."

I slid to the ground and thrust my pelvis in the air,
imagining the burnt sienna color Epic's eyes would be if
he were standing close enough to touch me. And, oh, how
I wanted him to touch me. I writhed on the ground, running my hands over my own body, pretending that soon
my touch would be replaced by Epic's firmer one.

The chorus slammed into me again and I quickly rose
to swing around the pole once more.

"I can't seeee—What will beee-come of me?"

The song came to an end soon after that with a few
instrumental bars and low unintelligible growls from Epic.
I finished up my first dance and as the music stopped I
blinked into the bright lights and focused on Tweedle Dee
and Tweedle Dum for the first time since Chameleon's
song had started. Both of them were silently staring at me,
mouths agape.

I swung my head back and forth between the two of
them, waiting for some kind of instruction or comment.

"Ummm…" I cleared my throat. "Do you want me to
do another song or—"

"You're hired!" Tweedle Dee and Tweedle Dum said
almost in perfect unison.

Pleased and yet surprised, I raised my eyebrows. "Okay."
I mean, I knew I was good, but I didn't think that even I
could win these two skeezes over with only one song.

Tweedle Dee hurried down from the DJ booth, his tight
pants displaying just how much he had liked my dance.
"We're going to make you a star, baby. A star!"

I grinned. Having the distinction of being a top money-
maker for guys like Tweedle Dee and Tweedle Dum would

keep them off my back for the time being. And that's all I would need, because it wasn't like I was sticking around for them to become emboldened enough to start propositioning me again.

I winked at Tweedle Dee, who was standing over by the bar looking a bit flustered as he tried to cover a wet spot on the front of his pants. "I'll see you later, boys." I waved and then turned to leave. Neither of them responded to me, but I heard the low murmurings of their voices as they no doubt discussed the money signs I had placed in their eyes.

My audition had taken less than twenty minutes, but I left the room with my head held high without any of my orifices having been violated.

Just before I pushed out the front door of the club, a large hand grabbed my arm and pulled me back into a rock-hard chest. "Careful, baby, there are cameras everywhere."

The hand relaxed and I turned to look up into Epic's pinched face.

"I was worried."

"I can take care of myself." Besides, Epic had definitely been there with me in spirit.

Epic's nostrils flared and he ground his teeth together before relaxing. I knew he was having an internal struggle. Finally, he sighed. "I know. So did you get the job? You weren't in there for very long."

I rolled my eyes. "Don't sound so happy about the prospect that I may not have been hired, because I was. My audition didn't take long because I wasn't going to give them any kind of sexual favors like they wanted."

Epic's eyes flashed red with his anger. He started to turn, but I snagged his hand. "Let it go. You can't go around beating the shit out of everyone that propositions me, especially in a place like this." I squeezed his hand and nodded to the door. "I know you only came early to watch out for me. Do you want to come with me for a bit before you actually have to work?"

Epic's eyes flipped through an array of colors before finally settling back to normal. "What do you have in mind?"

"Probably exactly what you do." I pushed through the door and ran at top speed for my aerial scooter, knowing that Epic wouldn't be far behind. Sure enough, just as I was about to hop on my scooter, Epic's arms wrapped around my middle and he swung me around while I tried to contain my laughter.

"Stop, the cameras," I said breathily.

Epic set me down on the ground begrudgingly and I slipped onto my scooter triumphantly.

"Race you." I turned the ignition and revved the engine.

"Nix, no! You're going to get yourself killed!"

"Who wants to live forever?" I called over my shoulder as I sped off. I laughed into the wind, loving the way it felt rushing against my overheated skin.

"Nix, slow the fuck down!" Epic snarled as he pulled up beside me and grabbed my handle bar to force me.

I rolled my eyes but was secretly pleased that he cared. "You're the one who bought the damn thing for me."

"And I'm seriously regretting that decision right now."

We paused at a stoplight.

"I bet I could change your mind." I batted my eyelashes and bit my lower lip. I leaned forward so I could whisper in his ear. "I might have a problem. I think I'm an adrenaline junkie or something, because I'm seriously worked up right now." I snaked my tongue out to run along the shell of his ear. "Now who can I get to help me out with my little issue? Surely not a stick in the mud like—"

Epic's mouth came crashing down over mine, effectively stealing my words. His scent enveloped me with a sense of comfort and at the same time revved up my hormones even more. I rocked forward and cupped his hard length through his pants.

"Get a room!" someone yelled with annoyance, following their words with an angry honk.

Epic and I pulled away from each other and laughed. "We should probably take this somewhere else. For no other reason than someone from the club might see us, if they haven't already."

"Yeah. Even worse, we may kill ourselves on the aerial highway." Epic pulled me back into him again.

"Epic—" I protested against his demanding lips.

Not until more horns began to honk did Epic finally disengage from our kiss.

"Come with me," he growled while sliding me over to his scooter until I was in front of him. In seconds, he changed gear and sped off. My scooter hovered in the area where I'd left it. He'd purchased upgrades when he bought the bikes. The upgrades included automatic security locks that shifted on whenever the floor panels sensed the driver was gone. Lots of people fell from scooters these days and instead of others helping them, the people snatched the poor saps' vehicles and fled.

My scooter should be safe from being stolen. People will just have to drive around it. Fuck them.

"Hold on, Nixie baby."

There was barely enough room for his large frame, so I was pushed up flush against him. He tucked my head under his chin and sped off.

I'd been under the impression that he was either going to take me home to his bed, or maybe even stop into a shady hotel, but even that wasn't fast enough for Epic's liking. He abruptly pulled off into a dark alleyway and bent me over the front of the scooter. In no time flat, my bare ass was in the air and he was sliding into me from behind. There was no use in me protesting. My level of wetness would tell him I was up for exactly what he was giving me. His fingers bit into my hips as he moved my body along his rock-hard dick. I felt like a teenager again, trying to get it wherever and however I could with my boyfriend. Just then Epic's palm slapped my ass and I moaned louder. *None of my boyfriends ever worked me over this good.*

"Nixie baby, fuck, you feel so good."

My thighs began to shake and I gripped the front of the scooter for fear of falling off. I was about to lose control and Epic was already long gone. "Nix, I'm close, I want to feel you come all around me—please, baby."

As if his words gave me permission, my orgasm ripped through my system and I screamed while I rocked back against him. I felt him climax mere moments later, accompanied with a strangled moan.

In the afterglow, while little aftershocks made my thighs quiver and Epic still held himself inside me—I wondered if maybe, possibly, Epic and I could make our relationship work and *if* I was falling for him. *Am I?* I wasn't even sure if I'd know it if I was. Things were moving so fast between us—impossibly fast. It was either the biggest mistake of my life—bigger than Teddy—or the best thing to ever happen to me. I was praying it was the latter.

CHAPTER 17
EPIC

Get your mind on the hit and off of Nix.

I rubbed my face. Her scent stuck to my fingers. I had to force myself to not lick them or allow my mind to linger to the moment on the scooter. *Fuck.* She felt so good, so soft, and all mine. My dick throbbed with the thought that I'd be lying next to her again that night.

Concentrate.

I headed down the staircase. Red screens decorated the walls. Each held a pre-recorded image of a naked woman gyrating. I opened the door to the bottom level. Perfume mingled with smoke. I couldn't figure out where the smoke was coming from—hash, tropic, or marijuana. *Maybe cigarettes.* People were reverting back to the old-time paper cigarettes stuffed with tobacco leaves instead of the electronic ones that heated the leaf with vapor. Music pounded, a hard-hitting guitar with a metaled bass.

Red light bathed the area. I was really starting to get tired of the color. It was all over this club and in the district.

It was hard to see with so many shades of red. But what I knew for sure was that women crowded the room and wore almost nothing but sweat and their hustle. Cube disks stuck to some of the dancers' breasts as if the guys sitting on the blood-red couches outlining the walls had slapped the money on those jiggling mounds. A DJ stood in the center inside a huge booth plastered with mirrors that reflected everything happening around him.

"Epic!" The blonde that Ain had brought over the night before ran up to me. A diamond bikini top strained to hold up her huge jugs. A diamond thong covered the area between her legs. She held an electronic cigarette between her fingers. Those candy-red lips widened into a huge smile. "Ain said you would start tonight. I've been looking all over for you."

"Why?" I stepped around her and scanned the area. Nix either danced on this level or the ones above it. I hoped for the higher one, not wanting any trouble since things between us were going good. Besides, the plan for the evening was to check out the club, familiarize myself with the layout, as well as search for weak points and hidden exits. I had no time for whatever this chick desired.

I glanced up. Glass served as the ceiling. Men fucked women on top of it. It was an orgy fest up there. Palms of different sizes pressed against the see-through ceiling. Knees smeared the glass as they moved within their own rhythm. Breasts bobbed. Fog misted some areas. White liquid squirted near the spot I stared at. *Nix better not be in that area.* I formed my hands into tight fists.

"So how do you like it so far?" the blonde yelled into my ear.

"What girls work up there?" I pointed to the ceiling.

"The ones that Rodney owns."

"Owns?"

She exposed the inner part of her wrist. Someone had embedded a barcode into her skin with digital ink. It gleamed in the red light. Earth had outlawed this form of slavery last year. Removing barcodes was big business.

"Trinity hasn't banned the slave trade here?"

"Nope." She placed her hand on my chest. "You're huge. I'm Ice, by the way."

"How many years do you owe?" I moved her hand away.

"Too many."

I directed my attention back to the ceiling showing the group sex. "So only slaves are up there?"

"Yes. Why? Are you thinking about buying one tonight? It's expensive and to even enter that level is half the mortgage on your average house."

"No." I forced myself not to curse as she returned her hands to my chest and slid them over the curves of my pecs. "I'm wondering if my cousin was placed up there."

"The new girl with the bird tattoo on her back?"

I nodded.

"No. She's over there." Ice gestured to my left. I zoomed my eyes into the area, shifted the light setting to bright, and spotted Nix instantly. Nix's gaze had already been focused on mine as she danced for the couple in front of her. A frown expanded across Nix's face when she looked at Ice's hands now fondling my abs. I shoved them away. Nix shifted her focus to the customers. The guy and girl pair appeared like the typical couple that would come to a club—fat, old-looking guy, sexy young lady. The guy stuffed a cube into the pocket garter on her thighs. His girlfriend giggled, raised her hands, and teased Nix's rosy-pink nipples. My dick jerked within my pants as Nix climbed on top of the girl and began to rock into her.

"Just your cousin, huh?" Ice laughed.

"Yes. Just my cousin." I battled with not licking my lips while the girl grabbed on to Nix's ass and squeezed.

"Well, at least that's what we want Rodney to think, right?"

I snapped my attention to Ice. "It's not what I want him to think. It's simply a fact."

She leaned into me, so that her sugar-scented perfume enfolded around me. Her lips brushed against my ear. "Ain isn't good at keeping secrets. Once his dick pushed into my mouth, he told me everything."

"Everything?" I feigned a bored expression, but inside fear swelled in my chest. *What the fuck did you say, Ain? I'm going to beat the shit out of you.*

"He told me that you all are planning a robbery here. The more I sucked, the more he said." Ice bit my earlobe. I tensed, mainly because I didn't want her touching me, but also because Nix's head turned my way and witnessed the nibble. Anger flickered in her eyes and she made no attempt to blink it away. Ice licked the side of my neck. "Ain promised me my freedom too."

"Back up." I shook her off me. "What do you mean 'your freedom'?"

"There's a safe near the exit that you all should escape from. Ain and I worked this change in the plan last night. While you are holding the place up, one of you, maybe your brother Shade or what-was-his-name—Toy, I think.

Maybe one of them can go into the safe and cancel out all of the slave contracts."

I scanned the area with my eyes. The music was loud. People focused on either getting money or being turned on, but still, I was uneasy about discussing this. "Is there somewhere private we can talk, a place without cameras?"

"All the way in the back of this level is an old changing area that isn't used anymore."

"Let's go." I motioned for her to show me the way.

She landed a peck on my cheek and sashayed off. Nix's gaze remained on me as we left and I hated that I couldn't explain. This chick Ice was dangerous. I had to get control of her. How, I didn't know, but something needed to be done. There was no way she was joining our group. I didn't trust her. I doubt Shade or Toy would be pleased, and with the way Nix scowled at Ice as I walked behind her, I didn't think Nix would support the idea either. *I'll have to pay her off to keep her mouth closed and probably promise to take away Rodney's claim of her.* After that, I planned to stomp Ain's dick into his center.

We arrived at a black door in no time at all. No bouncers lingered around. Ice opened the door for me and we slipped in undetected, at least I prayed no one saw. The music sounded faint from inside the closed room.

"I don't want any money just to be released from my barcode." Ice pushed a button. A white light came on above us. The room was huge. A few vanity tables were pushed up against each other on the side of the room. Racks of dresses rested on the other walls. Brown dust stuck to the pink carpet. Ice opened the front of her bikini top, snatched it off, and flung it my way. The diamonds clanked against each other when they fell to the carpet.

"And what do you want now?" I dug my hands into my pockets.

"I'd like to find out why they call you Epic." She stepped forward, tweaking her nipples with her fingers.

"It's short for my first name. Mystery solved." I leaned back on the wall, knowing where this was going. Ice had Ain wrapped around her little finger just by sucking his dick. She must have figured I was equally easy, maybe assumed she would spread those legs and I would do anything she asked. I let my view travel down her body. Ice's nipples perked up at the attention. Her body boasted decent-sized hips and a reasonably sexy pair of legs. Too bad Nix had destroyed me for any other woman. I doubted any other woman but Nix would be enough.

"Put your top back on. I'm not interested."

"'Cause of your fake cousin?" She wiggled her shoulders. Those breasts jiggled with the movement.

"Yes. My cousin is quite a woman. No other could do."

A muscle in her jaw twitched. "Why not have us both? I can keep a secret."

"I don't need another."

"Are you sure about that?"

"Definitely."

She pinched both of her nipples. A deep moan escaped her parted lips. "I bet you have a huge cock."

My dick hardened with a hint of interest. "Let's get down to business before I start to get mad."

She rolled her eyes. "I want my freedom."

"Okay. I want you out of this hit. I'll get you released and you leave the planet without a word about this hit. How do I get into the safe?"

"I have the code. All you have to do is—"

Nix burst through the door and slammed it behind her. One gun lay in each hand. One pointed at the center of my forehead. The other targeted Ice between her bare breasts. My dick went limp. My breath lodged in my throat. The only sounds that could be heard were the diamonds on Ice's thong clinking against each other as she shivered in fear and the erratic thumping of my heart as I tried to figure out a way to stay alive long enough to explain to Nix why we were in there.

Nix pressed both buttons on the butt of the guns with her thumbs, triggering the siphons to charge and prepare to be fired. "This is quite disappointing. And I have a tendency to get an itchy trigger finger when I'm disappointed. Care to explain, Epic *baaaby*?"

CHAPTER 18
PHOENIX

I ground my teeth together and tried to resist the very real urge to pull the triggers on both guns. I couldn't decide who deserved my anger more—Epic or the dumb slut who seemed determined to get underneath him.

You can trust me. Tell me what I need to do to prove it to you. I'll do anything. I'll be your anything. Just tell me what to do, Nixie baby.

Epic's words ricocheted around in my brain, and quite effectively stirred up even more anger in me, which I hadn't thought possible.

"This isn't exactly making me think I can trust you, Epic." I growled in response to his phantom words. "Or did you think that once I trusted you, I'd be more easy to fool?" My body began to shake. "You better start explaining, dammit!"

"Nixie—baby—please—look at me."

I flicked my gaze up to meet Epic's. His eyes met mine head on and without any signs of guilt that I could read. "Fine. Start explaining. Now."

I'd give him one chance to explain. One.

"I don't want her. I only want you. I can't control who comes on to me. I can only control my own actions."

"That doesn't explain why the fuck you came in here with her. If—"

"Ain fucking blabbed. She knows why we're really here. She wants to be a part of the hit."

The truth of the situation snapped into place. Oh, yeah, I knew her type. I swung both guns to point at the blonde slut's chest. I heard Epic exhale in relief and I chuckled. "And what—you thought you could fuck your way into control of him? Just like Ain?"

Her blue eyes widened with surprise.

"Answer me!" I hissed.

"I, well—I—"

"Spit it the fuck out!" I had absolutely no patience left. I was beyond sane thoughts at the moment. This stupid blonde slut thought she could seduce *my* man? The man that—yeah—I loved. *I love Epic. Shit.* I knew I was falling for him, or that I could fall for him, but it looked like I'd fallen.

"I just want my freedom!" the slut blurted out, the terror in her eyes increasing with every passing moment.

I smiled. "Your freedom, oh, is that all? What's your name?"

Some of the tension in her body expelled as she released a shaky breath. "Ice. My name is Ice."

"Well, Ice, today is your lucky day, because I'm about to give you your freedom." I pulled the triggers on both guns. The soft hiss of the siphons discharging into her chest echoed through the small space. Ice's eyes widened in shock briefly before they slid shut and her body slumped to the ground.

"Fuck!" Epic swore. "What did you just do?"

A weird sense of calm washed over me. "I thought it was obvious. I just iced Ice." Epic just stared at me and I wondered if I had effectively *iced* our budding relationship as well. He had to think I was completely insane. And hell, I kind of did too. I'd just killed someone because she was trying to seduce Epic. I could try to rationalize my motivations away and say she needed to die because she knew too much, but I would only be lying to myself.

"I'm sorry." Tears stung at the corners of my eyes. "I'm so sorry . . . I just blew all of our plans to high hell. I don't know . . . I couldn't . . . I love you. Of course you probably think I'm completely nuts now. And I couldn't blame you . . . I just . . ."

Epic stepped forward and palmed the back of my neck with his huge hand. "I already knew you were crazy, Nix. Maybe I am too, because—yeah—I fucking love you too."

My heart sped up as Epic pulled me into him, his lips slanting over mine. His tongue invaded my mouth and I savored the flavor of him that I thought just a second before I might never get to taste again. I was frantic for him.

Epic broke away from me and I whimpered.

"We have to take care of the body." He ran his hands through his long hair and grimaced. "Shit. Now I know why couples aren't permitted to work here together."

"What are we going to do?"

"I got this, baby. Alright? Just go back to work and I'll take care of everything."

"Epic, no. It's my mess. I can't let you—"

Epic dipped his head to press his lips against mine briefly. "We're in this together. Now give me those guns." I numbly handed them to him. He started wiping them clean of prints. "There aren't any cameras in here. We're just going to leave her in here. Alright? Now go back to work."

"So you're thinking we should just let her body be discovered?"

"Yeah, it's our best option. Although I'm also thinking we're going to have to push this heist forward a bit." Epic stared at the floor, deep in thought. "Yeah, it could just work."

"What?" I asked nervously, shifting from foot to foot.

Epic's eyes blazed with excitement. "We're going to do it tonight. We'll use her death as a distraction. It won't be as clean and pretty as we had wanted, but it'll have to do."

I bit my lower lip. "I'm sorry. I screwed up everything with my jealousy."

"No, Ain did when he started blabbing our secrets as soon as his dick found solace in Ice's mouth. Ain is the one to blame here, not you." Epic grinned at me. "Trust me, okay, Nixie baby?"

"Yeah. Okay." My fingers itched to run through his hair and pull him to me. I wanted him inside me so much it almost hurt. It didn't matter about the dead stripper on the floor. Nothing else mattered except for me and Epic.

"Don't look at me like that, baby," Epic said. "I don't think I'll be able to stop myself from fucking you right here if you don't stop."

"You're just as insane as I am." I stepped toward him and pushed my body into the length of his. Epic's erection pushed against my stomach through his pants.

"I don't think I can deny that." His hands slid down to cup my ass before he gently pushed me away from him. "We can't get caught in here. You need to get back to work and I'm going to find Ain."

"What do you want me to do about the rest? The heist and everything?"

"We're going to have to wing it, Nixie baby. You okay with that?"

"You know I am. I'll do anything for you." I glanced down at Ice's motionless body. Hell, I'd already killed someone for him. What was left?

Epic's gaze followed mine. "Yeah, I know. And I'll do anything for you, baby. You know that, right?"

I nodded once and ran my thumb over Epic's heart key nestled between my breasts. How could I have doubted him, even for a moment when I wore something so important to him around my neck?

"I'm sorry." I couldn't help but apologize again. I should have trusted him. What the hell had I been thinking? Well, really, that had been the problem—I *hadn't* been thinking.

"I don't want to hear you apologize again. I love you. Besides, doing the heist this way will probably be more fun." He grinned, but the humor didn't reach his eyes. "I need you dancing as close to the DJ as possible. I'm going to bust in . . . and . . . just follow my lead."

I couldn't help but laugh as I turned and left him to go back to my *job*. Again, I couldn't help but wonder if Epic was the best or worst thing to ever happen to me.

CHAPTER 19
EPIC

As soon as Nix left, I crumbled to the floor. Hard dick or not, I was rattled. She killed Ice, just like that, with no pause for thought. She pulled the trigger. Boom. Ice was dead. I'd soothed her the best I could. The whole time stress pounded against my temples and my erection pressed through my pants. My mind fogged into insanity and horniness. *She's making me crazy.* Even now I balanced on the edge of madness as Ice's corpse lay a few feet from me. My nose itched for quake. My fingers shook in terror.

How do I get us both out of this? Is there a way, or are we both already fucked? Any prehistoric robot could sniff a dead body out if the police were called. I'd heard that Trinity's security force owned high-tech androids. The planet's crime rate was the lowest in the galaxy. Even if I tried to hide the body, they'd discover the perpetrators.

I yanked out my phone, dialed Shade's number, and prayed to all the gods people kneeled to in time of need—the Duchess of Light, God, Jesus, Turpitude, etc. I crossed my fingers and closed my eyes as the phone rang three times.

Shade picked up on the fourth ring. I almost cried with joy. "Epic, everything okay?"

"No." I opened my eyes and gazed down at Ice's body. "In fact, things couldn't be worse."

I explained everything to Shade, from the moment Ice stepped to me until Nix left the closet. The whole time Shade cursed.

"Just get out of there, man," Shade said when I was done. "Grab Nix and head home. We all got to leave the planet tonight. Forget about the hit."

"Where in the darkness are we going to go?" I beat my hand against the door. "It was always about this hit. This was supposed to be the last one. Mimi would have money for college. The kids would be in better schools—"

"You stay there and you both will be dead or in jail. For murder, they'll put you on Saturn in the mines for life. You'll never see us again."

I rubbed my hands against my face. The music outside the door maintained a faint thump that boomed at the same fast rhythm of my heart. Not many options existed—run, jail, or death. Could Nix and I get away with the murder? I doubted it. Someone had to see Ice and me go in. It wouldn't have been a big deal if Ice was alive, but now that she was dead, if someone investigated it, then people's memories would be jogged. Even worse, someone had to spot Nix burst into the closet with two guns. Being that she'd come in full of rage, I didn't think she'd had the forethought to sneak in. She'd been pissed.

"Epic?"

"I'm thinking." I paced in the closet.

"There's nothing to think about."

"We don't have the money to run. We put most of it on the house and schools for three months. We got enough for two weeks maybe on a cheap planet, which means back to earth."

Shade cursed again and then said, "Nix shot her. Let Nix take the blame. Tell Ain and—"

"No! Don't even say anything like that again."

"But—"

"I'm serious. I brought her in with us, promising we'd watch her back. I'm not going to just let her get caught to save my ass."

"You mean to save all of our asses."

"Shade, forget it." I paused for a minute. "Fuck it. I might as well just say it. I love her, man."

"Are you fucking serious? You just met her."

"That being said, if Nix goes down, I go down with her."

Silence passed on the line. I hated to do this to him and hoped he understood that it wasn't the case of Nix over our family, but that Nix was part of the family now, even though she was a trigger-happy psycho. She was still all mine, and I loved every part of her, even the parts that scared the shit out of me and would possibly give me nightmares next week.

"What do you want me to do?" Shade broke the silence.

"Grab Toy and as many guns as you can—"

"What the fuck, Epic?"

"We're robbing Dynamics tonight. Nix and I. I need you and Toy to pick us up. We're on the bottom level now.

There is no way we'll be able to get up to the roof without being killed. Get to the back exit on ground level—"

"This is crazy. I have no idea where the back exit is."

"Ain will tell me. Trust me." I glanced at my watch. He had to be working right now. "Just head here with Toy and as many guns as you can get. Be here in no less than fifteen minutes."

"Fuck!"

"We'll run out. You shoot anyone chasing us. We jump in the car and you speed off."

"This is your grand plan?"

"For now it is." I hung up and dialed Ain's number. He answered after the first ring.

"Epic, my man," Ain said. "Are you finding everything okay downstairs?"

"No." I snatched an old dancer's outfit off a hanger and covered Ice's face. "I need you to meet me on the bottom level. You know where that abandoned closet is in the far back?"

"Of course. Most of the managers do our thing in there with some of the nicer girls." He laughed.

"Ice is here."

"Y-yeah," Ain stuttered. He had to know I realized he messed up.

"Come on down. As you've probably guessed, the plan has changed. I'll need your help with the new one."

"Gotcha."

I figured he would have taken longer, but he was more scared than I thought. It took him less than two minutes to arrive. He entered and shut the door. I snatched the costume off Ice's face. He screamed. I slapped him. My palm stung, but I bet his face hurt more.

He held the side of his face and pointed. "S-she's dead."

"And you basically killed her." I pulled out Nix's gun and rammed it in his mouth. "You told her about the hit man. Not a good idea. She thought she could suck me off and have me doing anything she wanted. What she never figured on, is me having a psychotic girlfriend who doesn't do well with females touching me."

Ain mumbled something incoherent with the gun in his mouth. Sweat trickled down his face. I slid the gun out of his mouth. His bottom lip quivered. "The black-haired girl killed Ice?"

"You're a smart one, aren't you? Is there an exit on this level?"

"Yeah. It's a secret."

"Now's the time to reveal it. We know you're not good with secrets, don't we?"

"I-it's next to this closet, but on the left further in the corner. You have to press the wall. A light comes on. It takes a thumb print to unlock."

"Your thumb work?"

"Yes, but what are you going to do with me? We're family, man." Water glazed over his eyes. Tears spilled out the corners. "I never had a way with ladies like you and Shade. I got to be the only guy who works in a strip club that almost never gets laid. When Ice approached me, I got a bit excited. Please don't kill me, Epic. Our mothers were sisters."

"Calm down. I kept the point of the gun targeted at his forehead. "Answer me this. Who all knows that I'm your cousin?"

"Almost all the owners and Ted. He trained you."

"The guy at the rooftop entrance?"

"Yeah."

"Are the owners here tonight?"

"No. They all left, took a ship to the World Series." Ain's attention centered on the gun. "They got box seats. Why are you asking man?"

"Because you're going to be my hostage." I kicked the door open and wrapped my arm around his neck, towing him out the door. "Stay close to me and keep your damn mouth shut."

He shrieked as I pulled him along.

"Party is over!" I shot a bullet into the floor. The music ceased. Everyone screamed. People jumped up and got ready to rush out. My fingers trembled. I hoped no one saw in the red light. "Stay where you are! My boys are coming down the stairs and anybody in their way is getting blasted with siphons."

A woman on the right screeched in horror. Increasing my speed, I dragged Ain, in a headlock closer to the DJ I needed to make sure I had a good view of the entrance. Guards and bouncers would be here soon. Movement came from the side. A fat guy with his dick sticking out of his open pants jumped up.

"Sit down and pull your money out!" I pointed my gun at him.

"Drop your gun." A male's voice sounded behind me and then a shot blasted. I turned around to see the man collapse to the ground. Nix stood behind him with a tiny gun in her hands.

How many guns did she bring into this place and when did she do it?

"I've got your back, baby." She winked.

"I'm lucky you're with me instead of against me."

"Very true."

"Pull out your money!" she roared and held a plastic trash bag. "We don't discriminate. All planets' currencies are welcome."

I laughed at her taking Toy's line. "Don't try anything special, guys or ladies. Let's keep this simple and quick. That way no one dies tonight and you can all go back to being teased by these lovely women. By the way, the ladies don't have to contribute, just the men."

"Fuck that!" Nix shook her head. "I don't discriminate. Everyone drops their money in the bag tonight. That means ladies, androids, men, and whatever else is in here."

I've created a monster or was she one already?

Either way it didn't matter. She was mine and I was hers. People piled in disks, cubes, flash drives with bank account info, and anything else Nix deemed was worthy of the bag. She traveled around the room in seconds. One guy she shot in the calf for taking too long. That guaranteed the rest of the people were ready for her when she arrived.

The entrance door opened. Without waiting to see who it was, I shot at the center. The siphon burned into Ted's chest. He cried out in pain and slumped down to the floor. I shot the guy behind him. "Nix, that's enough. Head to the back near the closet."

"We only got half!"

"Get your pretty ass in the back!" I shot another guy and began dragging Ain back with me. Four more men appeared at the entrance. We were fucked. I could feel our deaths in my heart and taste them on my tongue. The chances of us making it out of the club dropped to low. Toy and Shade being outside of the club right now was most likely impossible. That meant we'd have to run through the city—an area we were unfamiliar with.

"Drop the gun." One of the guards shot me in the arm. I gritted my teeth. Blood spilled and scented the air. Ain screamed. Crying out in rage, Nix blasted siphons his way. They left her gun in rapid motion. Smoke rose from the tip. Two guys dropped. Blood sprayed. Dancers fled the area, bumping into the rest of the guards.

"Come on, Nix!" I raced to the back and glanced over my shoulder to make sure she was following. She flipped off her heels and sped my way. I didn't move until she was in front of me. She clutched the bag to her chest. I shot a few siphons behind me, not even targeting anyone. I just wanted to cause hysteria in the crowd and I did. People jumped up and ran in all directions, pushing each other out of the way, knocking into the poor DJ, and trampling over the guards at the entrance.

"Open the door!" I yelled to Ain. Although his legs wobbled a little he tapped the area. The space lit up with a white glow in the shape of a door. A box appeared where a doorknob would be. He pressed his thumb there. A click sounded. The door opened. Cool air breezed in. Car horns blared farther away. Nix went through without being ordered. I shoved Ain in next. A shot bit into my lower side.

"Oh God!" My body banged into the wall. Blood spurted out of the wound. A gut-wrenching pain exploded in the area. I clenched my teeth. My vision blurred.

"No!" Nix pulled me through the door, screaming as she tugged. "Help me, Ain. Help me get him through, dammit."

Another siphon pierced my other side. It hurt so much. I coughed. Blood coated my tongue and leaked out of my mouth. "Just go, baby. I'll meet you there."

"Fuck you, Epic. I'm not going anywhere without you." She yanked at me until I was all the way through. I crashed into her and Ain. We all fell down on the sidewalk. I shut my eyes. Someone slapped my face.

"It's not time to sleep, damn you!" Nix cried. "Get up! We have to go, baby. Help me, Ain!"

He said something. Or maybe there were others around. I battled to open my eyes, but my eyelids wouldn't budge. I lowered into myself.

I tried to talk, but blood poured out of my mouth. I needed to tell her to leave. She was so stubborn. Although I couldn't see, I knew she was there, shaking me. Her fragrance enclosed me, that aromatic blend of jasmine and rose. God, I was lucky to have met her—if not for just a few days, I'd held her close to me, skin pressed against skin. I licked every inch of her body, tasting her sweetness, relishing in the soft moans that left her lips. She'd been mine and nobody else's.

I reached my hand out to touch her. Her silky strands slipped through my fingers. She pressed my hand against her face. It was wet. I prayed tears didn't coat her cheeks as a soothing darkness devoured me.

CHAPTER 20
PHOENIX

All my fault. This is all my fault. Why couldn't I have trusted Epic?

He'd given me no reason not to—not really. If I hadn't let my jealousy overcome me, then I wouldn't have killed Ice. Without her death, Epic wouldn't be laying in a pool of his own blood. I'd essentially taken two lives when I'd aimed my guns at Ice's chest and pulled the trigger. Maybe it was karma—maybe it was—*no*. Cold, hard determination replaced my feelings of remorse and agony. I wouldn't let this happen.

It wasn't too late. "You're not going to die on me, Epic! I won't let you."

I laid his head down on the ground and wiped my blood-slicked hands on my bare thighs. I then picked up a gun and swung it around to point at Ain, who was crouched a few feet away with his hands over his head, almost as if he hoped that would hide him from me.

"Get the fuck up, now," I barked the order at him, but instead of complying, he curled more into himself. "I said to get the fuck up now!"

Ain whimpered.

"You're going to stand the fuck up, and help me, goddammit! Or so help me, I'm going shoot off that limp piece of skin between your legs that you call a dick."

Ain whimpered again, but his only response was to move his hands from his head to cover his crotch. As if that would really do any good. I growled in frustration. I had no time for this kind of shit if I wanted to save Epic's life. Since, clearly, Ain wasn't going to be any good to me anymore, I aimed and shot him directly between his beady little eyes, even though they were currently squeezed shut. A small sense of satisfaction coursed through my system as I surveyed the strangely macabre scene his blood and brains made in the dim lighting.

The sound of sirens began to wail in the background and I took in a shaky breath trying to decide what the next step in my plan would be. That's when Shade suddenly appeared beside me.

"What the fuck happened?" His voice shook with emotion. "Is—is Epic dead?"

"No! But we need to get him out of here before he is."

"You killed Ain." Not a question, I noted. He disappeared into the shadows. I scanned the area, but couldn't see Shade.

"Yeah, he—"

Suddenly Shade snatched the gun from my hand. "You can explain later. FYI, I'm going to need you to not kill anybody else tonight. Ain was our cousin. We hadn't seen him in ten years and when we did, we found ourselves in fucked-up situations, so I won't shed any tears over his death, but Epic isn't as sick as you and I."

"If someone gets in the way of Epic surviving this, I'll kill them."

He ignored me. "We need to get the hell out of here before we all end up getting arrested."

I nodded in agreement. "We need to get Epic to a hospital."

Shade slid his eyes to my face and some unreadable emotion passed across his features. He picked up his phone and spoke into the space comm feature on it. "Toy, we need transportation. Now."

A moment later a hover car sped its way toward us, coming to a screeching halt inches from the roof. Toy took in everything much the way that Shade just had—with emotion, and yet detachment, at the same time.

"Help me get Epic into the car," I yelled.

Toy jumped from the driver's side and silently the three of us managed to get Epic's large body into the back seat. His breathing was shallow, his heartbeat barely audible—I knew we didn't have much time left. I pressed my smaller frame against Epic, hoping my presence would soothe him and that he might benefit from my little bit of body heat. "Hurry, please. He needs a doctor. Now!"

"I'll make the call." Shade jumped behind the driver's seat. The doors slid down by themselves as we sped off into the night.

Alarm bells went off in my head. "Make the call? What do you mean 'make the call'?"

"We can't take him to a hospital, Nix." Toy stared at the ground. "Even if they manage to patch him up, that'll only be to ship him off to some kind of prison on probably one of the shittiest planets in the galaxy. He wouldn't want to live that way."

Fear shot up my spine and I shuddered. "What are you saying? That you're just going to let him die?"

"Of course not." Shade gripped the steering wheel so hard white formed around his dark knuckles. "But no hospitals. We know someone who can hopefully get the job done."

Hopefully?

"Who?" I was starting to panic. "Is he any good? Just tell me!"

"Calm down, Nix. He's our brother. We don't want him to die." Toy dialed out a number on his phone. "Epic found a doctor here before we even moved, just in case the kids got sick."

"Can this doctor take care of siphon wounds?"

"We'll see." Toy gritted his teeth and began to talk into the phone.

I listened numbly as his voice droned on, obviously explaining Epic's circumstances to their on-call doctor. I tried to calm myself. Toy was right. Epic was their brother. Of course they didn't want him to die. They'd do everything in their power to save him. But what if it wasn't enough? What if I lost the only good thing I had in my life? *No, no, no, no—NO!* I ran my fingertips through Epic's bloody and matted hair. My nostrils flared with the copper scent of his blood. My stomach clenched with nerves.

"It's not good enough," I whispered.

Epic could have turned his back on me when I killed Ice, saved himself. But he loved me with all his heart, the one that I held the key to around my neck. *What would he do if it was me lying broken and bloody in the back seat of this hover car? Would he let some second rate hack try to save me? No, he'd do everything in his power to keep me alive. And I'd do the same for him.*

I seized the gun out of Shade's holster and aimed at the back of Shade's black head. "It's not good enough."

"What the—?" Toy started but I didn't let him finish.

"You can hang up the phone now, Toy, because Epic isn't going to get second-rate medical attention from some guy that may or may not know anything about saving lives. We're going to a hospital."

"If you shoot me, we'll crash, and probably all be dead," Shade growled.

"Don't try to call my bluff, because I'm not bluffing. I know very well that if I pull this trigger, we'll crash and probably all die. That's why I pointed it at you and not Toy. It was the best motivation to reign you both in since I don't have two guns at the moment."

Toy narrowed his eyes at me and swore under his breath. "I really don't think she's bluffing, man. She's fucking insane."

Shade snorted. "Tell me something I don't know."

"If it makes me insane to love your brother so much that I'd do anything—risk anything to save him, then, yep, I am. Now drive us to the closest hospital. I don't care which one."

I wasn't quite sure what I planned on when I got Epic to whichever hospital Shade was racing us to, but I knew most of the medical facilities were hands and feet above even the best ones back on earth. Horns honked at us as we sped through the air. I kept my arm outstretched, holding the gun tightly against Shade's skull as I tentatively glanced at Epic's still unmoving form. I was petrified that despite everything, I still might be too late.

"Faster!" I screamed. "Drive fucking faster!"

"I'm going as fast as this piece of shit will go," Shade snapped.

My breathing came in short little spurts. My skin felt on fire and tears streamed down my face.

"Please, Epic baby, don't leave me." I pleaded as my body began to shake.

I can't lose him. I just can't.

"I think she's losing it," Toy muttered low as if I couldn't hear him.

I turned my face toward him and laughed without humor. "If you think I've already lost it, then you really don't want to see what's going to happen if Epic dies."

The United Ladies of Light hospital loomed in front of us, and the giant illuminated medical sign burned through the dark night like a promise of redemption. Shade zoomed up to the emergency entranceway and some staff hurried out to us.

I slid the gun behind my back and stood. "He's been shot. Please help him."

One of the nurses with reddish-orange skin—most definitely not human—addressed me. "Does he have insurance?"

I glanced in Toy's direction and he shook his head at me. "Ummm . . . no, I don't—"

The nurse raised her hands in the air. "We can't take him here then. If you take him over to—"

"He won't make it!" I screamed.

"I don't make the rules." The nurse looked at me with sympathy but still backed away from the car.

I produced the gun from behind my back and pointed at the nurse's head. "New rule. You're going to save his life if you want to live."

"Oh fuck," I heard Toy exclaim.

The nurse's red eyes widened with terror. She eyed my state of panic, then the gun, and then her gaze slid to Epic. She nodded, clearly understanding I wasn't giving her much of a choice.

I kept a close eye on the nurses as I waved the gun around to keep them moving. They rolled Epic through the hospital and down a long corridor. A short and stocky doctor appeared in front of us and frowned at me.

"What's going on?" he demanded.

I pointed the gun at him and he took in a deep, shuddered breath. "You're going to save him. That's what's going on."

He glared at me defiantly. "You're going to jail when this is over."

"I don't care. Just fix him." Nothing mattered besides saving Epic's life.

I numbly followed after the small team of doctors and nurses as they prepared for surgery. They each stepped under the disinfecting powder wash before donning gloves and masks. The material used for both shrank to fit snuggly over the flesh and was made out of a special material that fit like a second skin and yet permitted them to breath naturally. It had the effect though of making them seem as though all their mouths and noses had been spackled over with skin. It made me feel as if I were in some weird horror movie.

I hate hospitals.

I pushed down the memory of being brought to one after I escaped Teddy. I had no recollection of how I'd gotten there, just the vague recollection of stumbling into the ER bloody, bruised, and burned. I had been delirious from all the pain Teddy had inflicted on my body. The "mouthless" doctors and nurses had driven me into a panic and they had been forced to use sedation just to treat me.

But that wasn't an issue with Epic. He hadn't moved since he'd passed out on the roof, and a feeling of dread was beginning to constrict my throat. I leaned against the wall, tightly gripping the gun in my hand, and shivered as I watched the hospital staff begin to work on Epic. Monitors beeped, 3D screens appeared and disappeared, and the head surgeon barked orders with an authoritative tone.

"Get me ten cc of general coagulant and another of the synthetic universal blood." Nurses scurried around like bees swarming in a hive. "Get me a canister of nanobots. He's not going to make it without them."

The gun rattled in my hand. I continued to shiver from the low temperature in the operating room, but I couldn't leave Epic, despite the fact I was almost naked and covered in blood. I must have appeared insane. *Good, because I am.*

"He's going into cardiac arrest—"

"I have his heart key!" I exclaimed, snapping my full attention back to what was happening with Epic. I rushed forward and slid the chain from around my neck and thrust it at a short nurse with brown hair. Her eyes met mine briefly with sympathy before she turned and handed it to the doctor.

The familiar mapping that Epic had shown me the night he'd given me the key appeared in the blank space above him. The doctor seemed to recognize the problem immediately. "We need specialized heartbots—stat! His faulty valve can't take the stress of what's happening to the rest of his body. It takes precedence."

My vision began to darken around the edges and I struggled to stay upright on my feet. I felt so tiny and helpless despite the power wielding a gun gave me. There was only so much even these doctors and nurses could do for Epic if his body gave out on him. The medical technology of our day was amazing, but it wouldn't work any actual miracles.

Shade, as usual, seemed to appear out of nowhere and suddenly he was standing beside me. He placed a large warm hospital blanket with automated heating around my shaking shoulders and stared straight ahead at the commotion surrounding Epic.

"I love my brother. You know that, right?"

I nodded blankly. "He loves all of you too."

"He loves you too, Phoenix. He told me as much and I thought I should tell you in case he—"

I clutched the gun tighter in my hand. "He's not going to die. I won't let him."

"He won't survive in whatever jail they put him in—if he lives. I'm sure you've already figured out that my brother is softer on the inside than he appears."

Tears dripped down and bypassed the weak smile that spread across my face. "I won't let him go to jail either. I'm going to take him far, far away from here and we'll spend the rest of our days lounging on sandy white beaches and drinking cocktails—like in the movies. I'll spend the rest of my days making him forget all of his pain. I'll make him happy." My face scrunched up and I started to cry some more, not the calm tears, but the loud, ugly-faced, throat-choking ones. "Oh please, Duchess of Light, give me the chance to make him happy."

Looking uncomfortable, Shade draped an arm around me and pulled me into his side. I continued to sob, not caring that my tears were seeping into Shade's T-shirt. "There are enforcers surrounding the building. We're fucking lucky that we happened to find the one religious hospital near the Red Light District. It's illegal for enforcers to step on holy ground. Do you have a plan?"

"It won't matter if he doesn't make it," I said between sobs. Soon I cried myself to sleep in Shade's supportive arms.

I awoke to the steady murmurs of the machines monitoring Epic's heart and lung function. One of the siphons had exploded in his chest and collapsed a lung. The doctors had done all they could and we were just waiting for the nanobots inside his system to hopefully finish the job of repairing him. The technology would normally be out of Epic's reach, but a crazy woman wielding a gun filled to the brim with siphons was the same thing as a blank check.

I hadn't left Epic's side for longer than it took to grab some clothes from the gift shop and to clean up a bit. I didn't want Epic to panic when he woke because I was covered in blood and he would be waking up anytime now.

I leaned over his sleeping form and pressed my lips to his forehead. "Can you hear me, baby? Please come back to me. I need you. We need to come up with a plan to get out of here and I can't do that with you playing Sleeping Beauty."

When he didn't respond, I sat back down and slipped my hand around his. "Epic—please."

Fresh tears spilled down my face. After all I'd shed, I thought I'd gone dry by now, but I guess when it came to Epic, I would always have a reserve. I bowed my head and pressed my face into Epic's hand. His scent was absent and only the combination of disinfectant and the metallic nanobots lingered on his skin.

"Aww, Nix. I never pegged you as the dramatic type."

I jerked up and my watery eyes met Epic's baby blues. I let out a very girly squeal and launched myself at him. "Epic! I thought you were going to die!"

I buried my face in Epic's hair as his arm came up to wrap around me slowly. "I think—I think I was dead for a minute. I saw you and Shade, and you were crying." He ran his hand through my hair. "I felt so peaceful, and I think—yeah—I think I saw my parents."

I remained silent and just listened to the voice I thought I might not ever get to hear again.

"But seeing Mom and Dad wasn't what I wanted. I think I turned back somehow. I came back for you. Only for you."

There were so many things I wanted to say to him, but there would never be enough time. So I settled for the most important. "I love you."

"Yeah, I know, Nixie, and I love you too." His gaze roamed me from top to bottom "You look good. I'm glad nothing happened to you. Did Ain make it out safely? Did he get shot too?"

"I shot him."

"You shot him?"

"Yes."

"He's dead?"

"Yes."

He closed his eyes for a few seconds and sighed. "Have you killed anyone else?"

"No."

"We'll have to deal with Ain's death later, but sadly, you can't get rid of me that easily. Based on that truth, I wonder who's crazier, me or you?" He blew out a long breath. "Can you promise to not kill anyone else?"

"I'll do my best." I pulled away from him and studied his unreadable face. "How are you feeling?"

"Weak still, but I'm alive. So what else did I miss?" He tossed a weak grin at me and I shook my head.

"A lot."

A little while later, after I had filled Epic in on the, well . . . *epic* mess I'd made out of everything, he told me he wanted to see Shade and Toy. They were right outside the door and they greeted him with both joy and trepidation as we began to discuss what we would do now that Epic was out of the woods health wise.

"Toy, Shade," Epic's voice shifted to an uncompromising tone, "you need to take care of the rest of our family. We can't all go down."

As the brothers argued, a plan began to take shape in my mind.

CHAPTER 21
PHOENIX

Epic followed along behind me slowly. All his strength hadn't returned yet.

"Do you trust me, Epic?"

"Yeah, you know I do. But what about the nanobots? What'll happen if they aren't extracted?"

"I read an article once that claimed nanobots, if left inside the human body, would lay dormant and only become activated when they were needed. Like if you get another injury or something."

Epic quirked a blond eyebrow. "So in theory—I'm invincible now?"

I rolled my eyes. "I wouldn't go that far. But my point is, they're not keeping a super close eye on you because they don't think you'll try to leave before they can extrac the bots. They probably think you're too scared."

"I won't lie, I am a bit nervous leaving them in. W if that article was a crock of shit?"

"It's this or some kind of prison . . ." I let my voice trail off, not wanting to say the rest. We'd never see each other again if that happened. Death would be a much gentler punishment. "And besides, at least this way Toy and Shade won't be blamed for any of this. They'll get off scot-free and Mimi and the gang won't have to suffer any more than they already have.

"Where are we anyway?" Epic whispered.

"They've been doing construction on the bottom few floors of the hospital—renovations, which is very convenient for us. We just need to get outside and steal a hover car to make our getaway."

"And then what? They're going to chase us. This planet is only so big."

"You just let me worry about that."

Epic grunted, but I took that as a yes. Once outside, stealing an enforcer car wasn't as difficult as I'd expected. There were tons of cop cars around, and no one would expect us to take one of those, that was for sure. I grabbed harner jackets from the trunk just in case we crashed. All enforcement vehicles kept extra pairs in the back. Each jacket had a parachute lined inside, first-aid kit, breathing device, and packets of dehydrated food for a week. The theory was that if a person fell into space and landed on a planet, that person could survive for a week. Too bad I never discovered what would happen after a week was up.

I may need that information right now.

"I already knew you were nuts, but, baby, this one takes the cake," Epic muttered under his breath as I slid into the driver's side of the cop car I had chosen for our target. "And why do you get to be the one to drive?"

"Because I said so and you're about to pass out from just traveling to the vehicle." Putting on my jacket, I handed one to him. "Now put on this jacket."

"What's this?"

"It's in case we crash and have to evacuate."

"Are you planning on crashing?" He slipped it on. His face cringed a few times as if it hurt for him to move too much.

"I'm not planning on crashing, but I damn sure am not planning on stopping." I turned my attention to the dash in the car and shook my head in bewilderment. "I can't believe they don't even have it locked or coded."

"That's because they don't think anyone is stupid enough to try and steal one right out from under their noses."

Nervous anticipation caused my heart to thrum loudly as I pushed the button to turn the car on. The engine hummed to life and the dashboard lit up with a bevy of tech stuff, half I'd never even heard of. Locating the drive button, I punched it next and sucked in a deep breath as I began to slowly steer the car away from the hospital. *We're doing it. We're really doing it.* My nerves quickly turned to excitement as the hospital appeared in the rearview sensor screen.

But I'd gotten a little cocky too fast. Suddenly a spotlight shone down into my eyes from above. "Halt where you are."

Lights began to flash and the red, blue, and purple enforcer lights illuminated the dark night sky.

"Fuck!" Epic swore.

"No," I said between clenched teeth. "I'm not stopping and I won't lose you. We've both suffered too much in our lives and come too far to give up now."

Epic's gaze swung to mine and his eyes flicked through a myriad of colors before settling back on their normal cool ice blue. Determination settled into every line in his face. "I'm with you, Nixie baby, and I will be until I take my last breath and probably beyond that."

I smiled at him like a maniac and hit the button that threw our ride into top gear. We sped off into the night with at least two-dozen enforcer cars on our tail. I let out a high-pitched squeal of excitement. My adrenaline had all my senses on hyper alert, and some sick, twisted part of me was enjoying myself.

"Where are we going?"

"Where ever we can get!" I increased the speed and cried out with unabandoned joy.

"You're beautiful when you lose it." Epic laughed. "Scary too, but also captivatingly beautiful."

I dodged traffic signals, aerial transports, and other commuters as we attempted to make our getaway. I was hoping that eventually the enforcers would give up, but I knew better. After all, my father had been one and it took a certain type of dedication to the Duchess to become one. They were all fanatics and would probably chase us to the ends of the planet.

Our luck had been going fairly well until an older woman drove out into the intersection in an older hover craft. I had to veer suddenly to the left and it sent us careening toward a cluster of buildings. I tried to turn the wheel more, but I saw what was coming and we were about to go splat.

I glanced over at Epic and I saw him realize the same thing. Left with no other choice, another crazy idea came to me. "We have to jump."

Epic's mouth dropped open, but then he nodded. "Not much else to do."

"Maybe we'll get lucky, maybe we'll survive."

"Maybe, but if we don't . . ." He grinned at me. "Who wants to live forever anyway? My dad told me to never fall in love with a girl you can't live without. I can't live in this fucked-up galaxy unless you're by my side, so if we die tonight, I'll die a happy man."

I grinned back at him and reached for the bag containing the money from our disastrous heist. I refused to leave it just in case we did make it. It was blood money, mostly Epic's, and I wasn't going to let him not get his payoff. I opened the escape hatch on the bottom of the car and laced my fingers with Epic's. He leaned over and kissed me briefly, because there wasn't time for anything else. And then we jumped.

EPILOGUE
PHOENIX

"*The bodies of Teresa Marie Folino and Epicaderous Malleous Brownstone were never found. Some claim they were incinerated in the fiery explosion caused from the enforcer car hitting the side of the credit building, but others—well, others of the more romantic breed believe that somehow they survived. Some claim to have made sightings in the Serrion district. Others say—*"

I switched the viewing screen off and snorted. "As if I would be caught in a place like Serrion district. I'm far too rich and snooty for that now."

I chuckled to myself as I padded barefoot onto the deck where my husband was strumming his favorite acoustic guitar while gazing off at the rising of our planet's five moons.

"Hey." His lips formed into a smile, one I wanted to kiss and devour right there on the patio.

"Hey, yourself." I curled up in his lap. He made room for me by setting his guitar next to his leg. Moonlight hit his skin and reflected off his artificial eyes. He wrapped his arms around me and we sat in contented silence.

Somehow we'd made it. We'd risen up from the ashes of our horrid pasts and found our redemption in each other's hearts. We were both like the phoenix in my tattoo now. Both of us had risen from our seemingly eminent deaths and had walked away stronger, better—re-birthed. It hadn't been easy for Epic to leave everyone and everything behind. But it had been the only way. Although I had a feeling anonymous donations would be appearing in his family's bank account once some more time passed.

Epic's generous heart was one of the many things I loved about him. The other, well—no other man had ever made me so hot for him. He was my savior and my hot—hot redemption. He was my everything.

"What are you thinking about, Nixie baby?" Epic's low voice rumbled against my ear.

I twisted around and straddled him. "Oh, just about how you're my hot, sexy redemption."

"Does that even make sense?"

"Of course." I tapped my chest. "I said it."

"I never would have pegged you for such a corny, romantic sap. But you are, aren't you, baby?"

I stuck my tongue out at him. Without hesitation, he captured it and sucked into his mouth, effectively blanking my mind of everything but him.

ABOUT THE AUTHOR

K.D. Penn is a pseudonym for the writing team of authors Kenya Wright and D.T. Dyllin.

KENYA WRIGHT

Kenya Wright resides in Miami with her three amazing, overactive children, a supportive, gorgeous husband, and three cool black cats that refuse to stop sleeping on her head at night.

Other Dragonfairy Press books by Kenya:
Fire Baptized
The Burning Bush

D.T. DYLLIN

Cynical-Optimist. Chocolateholic. Sarcasm Addict. Paranormal Believer. Self-Imposed Insomniac. Sci-Fi Geek. Animal Lover. Writer . . . are just a few words to describe D.T. Dyllin. She was born and raised in Pittsburgh, Pennsylvania, and now lives in Nashville, Tennessee, with her husband and two very spoiled German Shepherds.

Other Dragonfairy Press books by D.T.:
Hidden Gates
Broken Gates
Feeling Death